WILLIAM ALEXANDER

NOMAD

MARGARET K. McELDERRY BOOKS
New York   London   Toronto   Sydney   New Delhi

para mis sobrinos Kyla y Rory

MARGARET K. McELDERRY BOOKS * An imprint of Simon & Schuster Children's Publishing Division * 1230 Avenue of the Americas, New York, New York 10020 * This book is a work of fiction. Any references to historical events, real people, or real places are used fictitiously. Other names, characters, places, and events are products of the author's imagination, and any resemblance to actual events or places or persons, living or dead, is entirely coincidental. * Text copyright © 2015 by William Alexander * Jacket illustration copyright © 2015 by Stéphanie Hans * All rights reserved, including the right of reproduction in whole or in part in any form. * MARGARET K. McELDERRY BOOKS is a trademark of Simon & Schuster, Inc. * For information about special discounts for bulk purchases, please contact Simon & Schuster Special Sales at 1-866-506-1949 or business@simonandschuster.com. * The Simon & Schuster Speakers Bureau can bring authors to your live event. For more information or to book an event, contact the Simon & Schuster Speakers Bureau at 1-866-248-3049 or visit our website at www.simonspeakers.com. * The text for this book is set in Adobe Caslon. * Manufactured in the United States of America * 0815 FFG * 10 9 8 7 6 5 4 3 2 1 * CIP data for this book is available from the Library of Congress * ISBN 978-1-4424-9767-2 (hardcover) * ISBN 978-1-4424-9769-6 (eBook)

FIRST
EDITION

Hope has two beautiful daughters
named Anger and Courage;
anger at the way things are,
and courage to see that they do not remain the way they are.

—Saint Augustine

PART ONE
REFUGEES

1

Zvezda Lunar Base: 1974

Nadia Antonovna Kollontai, the ambassador of her world, was not on her world.

She went walking on the moon. Sunlight bounced off the gray stone around her. She felt intense warmth through her bulky orange suit. The reflected glare blotted out all other stars. It turned the sky into absolute darkness. That felt close and comforting rather than infinite, as though Nadia had hidden both herself and the moon underneath a very thick blanket.

She looked forward to throwing that blanket aside.

"Nadia?" Her radio crackled and sputtered. "Zvezda base to Ambassador Nadia . . ."

"Hello, Envoy," she said.

"By my count your oxygen is running low." The Envoy

spoke Russian, and sounded exactly like her uncle Konstantine. It had borrowed Uncle's voice to seem familiar, familial, and comforting. It did sound familiar, but not especially comforting. Uncle Konstantine and Aunt Marina had had many practical virtues between them, but neither one of them had ever learned how to be comforting.

"Probably," she said, as though she didn't care how much air she had left. This wasn't actually true. She had kept careful tabs on her oxygen.

"Please cut short your unnecessary moonwalk and come back inside."

"On my way," she said, but she circled back the long way around to give herself more room to run.

Nadia took huge and sailing lunar leaps, gaining speed. She felt like she could push herself clear of the moon entirely if she only kicked hard enough. She felt like she could fly through space as her own ship.

She took several smaller steps to slow down when the Zvezda base came back into view.

Gray-and-beige modules of the station lay half-buried in lunar dirt. The dirt was supposed to protect the modules from radiation and small meteors, and maybe it did protect the half that was actually covered, but the robotic shovel had broken before finishing the job. Now it looked like a ruin, a relic of some ancient space age rather than the cutting, rusting edge of Soviet engineering.

Nadia tried not to be cynical about it. The moon base functioned well enough. She lived there. She breathed and ate there. But Nadia was from Moscow, and asking a Muscovite kid to be anything other than cynical about grand Soviet accomplishments was like asking fish to have eyelids. Besides, Aunt and Uncle had designed most of this place (though only Uncle actually got credit for it), so even though Nadia was proud of their astro-engineering, she had also overheard enough dinnertime grumblings about shoddy shortcuts to know that Zvezda barely held itself together with string and spit. And Nadia loved sarcasm. She loved how it could make any word mean both itself and its opposite.

"Nadia?" the Envoy asked, borrowed voice crackling over the radio. She imagined it peering through curved window glass in one of the unburied base modules, craning a long, purple neck to look for her. "Nadia, have you reached the airlock yet?"

"Not yet," she said, her voice pitched to soothe the worried Envoy. "But I can see it from here. Just a few minutes away."

"Stop," the Envoy insisted. "Stop right there. Don't come any closer. Find something to hide behind."

Nadia shuffled to a stop and looked around. She stood on a flat, featureless stretch of rock with nothing at all to hide behind. "What's wrong?"

"The Khelone ship is here. It is landing soon. It is landing *immediately*. I told you this would be a bad time to go for another idle walk."

"Fantastic," she said, and made the word mean both itself and its opposite. "You said it would be here soon as in *days*, not soon as in *minutes*." She was already running, each step a lunar leap.

"Don't pretend that the word *soon* is more precise than it really is," the Envoy told her. "Have you found cover yet?"

"Maybe." She spotted a small crater, a hole in the face of the moon where some small rock had smacked into it, months or centuries or millions of years ago. She skidded while shifting direction, took two more leaps, reached the crater—and sailed right over it. She had to take several small stutter steps to slow down and double back. Then she hopped into the shallow hole.

Nadia stood still, caught her breath, and finally looked up.

She saw the Khelone ship. It was the only visible thing in the sky besides the sun itself.

"Looks like a barnacle," she said.

"Apt comparison," said the Envoy. "Khelone ships are

living things. The pitted outer hull is a grown shell. Are you somewhere safe?"

"I think so," Nadia said. "Mostly. Probably."

The Envoy made a *pbbbbbbt* noise of nervous exasperation. "The force of the Khelone landing will throw a wave of dust and stone in all directions. One of those stones might shatter your helmet, or puncture your suit. That would be almost fitting. We survived a harrowing rocket launch, nearly exploded before we left the atmosphere, and barely managed to land out here. You have lived through impossible dangers already. Now you might be killed within sight of safety, by the very ship you summoned here, because you couldn't resist another unnecessary moonwalk."

"Can't bite your own elbow," Nadia said. It was one of Uncle Konstantine's expressions, and meant essentially the same thing as "so close and yet so far." He always said it with a shrug. Uncle had had lots of expressions, as though he were in some sort of hurry to become a folk-wisdom-dispensing old man—which would never happen now. He had lived long enough to become grumpy, but not long enough to be old.

Nadia turned her thoughts around to walk carefully away from memories of Uncle Konstantine and Aunt Marina.

"I have no elbows, Ambassador," the Envoy said with Uncle's voice.

She tried to crouch down in the crater. It wasn't easy. Cosmonaut suits did not lend themselves to crouching. "Say something nice. I might be about to die, and then your scolding complaint about elbows will be the last thing I'll ever hear. How sad. Say something nicer than that."

"Keep your head down, Nadia," the Envoy said. "Please don't die."

The Khelone ship threw a burst of energy at the ground to slow itself. That kicked up a wave of dust and stone, which expanded outward from the landing site in silence. Nadia tried to keep her head down, but small stones still smacked into her suit and helmet.

She had very carefully appropriated this suit before coming to the moon. It had once belonged to Valentina Tereshkova, the first female cosmonaut—and, prior to Nadia's flight, the only female cosmonaut. At that moment Nadia worried more about damaging the space suit of Valentina Tereshkova than she worried about dying from the damage. She idolized Valentina. The cosmonaut had repaired and reengineered her Vostok spacecraft *while already in orbit*. It never would have landed again otherwise. That was an embarrassing state secret, but Nadia came from a family of rocket engineers so she knew about it anyway.

The small, pelting debris settled down. Nadia didn't hear any hissing noises from Valentina Tereshkova's borrowed suit.

"Nadia?" the Envoy asked, worried.

"Still here," she said.

"Excellent," said the Envoy. "Now please hurry back. Try to reach the station before our guest does."

Nadia Antonovna Kollontai was born on April 12, 1961. Yuri Gagarin launched into space on the same day. He was the first human to do so—or at least the first to come home again afterward.

In 1969 Nadia became the ambassador of Terra and all Terran life. She was eight years old at the time. Ambassadors are always young. She lived with her aunt and uncle, and she handled intergalactic incidents on behalf of her planet. She did so in secret. Most human ambassadors do.

Meanwhile her aunt Marina and uncle Konstantine worked on the Zvezda base. Americans had just landed on the moon, so lunar goals had fallen out of favor in the Soviet space program. Uncle Konstantine convinced his project leaders to send a few rockets and drop a few modules of moon base by remote control, but the project ended there. Zvezda sat unfinished, unoccupied, and already abandoned.

Then Ambassador Nadia needed an off-planet site to arrange a meeting and hitch a ride.

She stowed away aboard the last N-1 rocket to Zvezda in August 1974. After that she spent more than a month eating cosmonaut food from toothpaste tubes, taking long moonwalks, and waiting for the Khelone ship to arrive.

Up close it still looked like a towering barnacle.

Nadia wondered what it was like to swim through space the way fish swam in water, no barrier between yourself and all the nothing that there ever was. She wondered what it was like to be a living ship. Then she stopped wondering so she could wrestle with the Zvezda airlock latch. It opened on the third try. Nadia climbed through the airlock, sealed both the outer and the inner doors, and then lifted her helmet visor.

The entrance module looked like the body of an airplane without passenger seats. It did not look hospitable or welcoming. It was a mess, an inauspicious place to make first contact. Engineers had no sense of ceremony. The ones in her family didn't, anyway, and she expected other engineers to be pretty much the same.

The Envoy scootched across the metal floor. It raised up its long neck and puppetlike mouth.

"Ambassador," it said, borrowed voice dryly formal.

"Envoy," Nadia answered. "Have you heard anything from our guest?"

"Not yet."

Nadia nodded. Then she started to pace. She could see the Khelone ship outside, through the module's single actual window. The opposite side of the module held a video screen pretending to be a window, one that showed looping footage of a scenic mountain view. Someone back home—definitely not Uncle Konstantine, but someone else on his team—believed that artificial scenery would benefit homesick cosmonauts. Nadia didn't find the fake window beneficial. She tried to ignore it.

"Please stand still," said the Envoy.

"I'm thinking," said Nadia.

"Must you always walk while thinking?" the Envoy asked. "Does your brain even work without the kinetic motion of your feet? You're making me nervous." It tinkered with a lumpy piece of machinery in its nervousness. "I hope the translator works. I did the best I could, but we have only so much equipment to work with here. Visual information may be distorted."

"We'll make do," said Nadia. "But stop fiddling around. You're just going to break it."

She expected the translation device to break anyway. She had expected the rocket that brought them here to explode on the launchpad. She inherited this kind of cheerful hopelessness from Aunt and Uncle—especially from Aunt Marina. "Engineers, rocket scientists, cosmonauts; they all know that things will probably break, fall over, and explode," her aunt would say. "But they're always so happy to be wrong."

Something knocked on the outer hatch of the airlock.

"Poyekhali," Nadia said. "Here we go."

2

Nadia resealed her helmet and climbed back inside the airlock, closing the inner door behind her.

She had met aliens before. She was an ambassador. Her whole job was to meet and communicate with the representatives of alien civilizations. But none of those meetings had ever happened in person. Nadia had never spoken with one of her colleagues while actually awake. Ambassadors used very strange physics to dream themselves elsewhere. They met in the Embassy, in the very center of the galaxy, without actually having to physically travel—which was good, because it would take many thousands of years to travel so far, even at the speed of light.

Unless you knew how to take shortcuts.

The knock came again. Nadia opened the outer door.

A turtle-shaped suit climbed inside on four legs. It

kicked the door shut with one hind leg, stood up, and considered Nadia through a dark helmet visor. She considered it back. Then she reopened the inner door and gestured inside.

In the Embassy, while dreaming Embassy dreams, Nadia's fellow ambassadors looked human to her. Communication always required more than words. Facial expressions, gestures, postures, behaviors, and games all needed translation, so her colleagues always looked human. Nadia would see them smile, frown, and wave hands in familiar sorts of ways. But she had also learned how to squint and sneak secret glances at the *actual* shapes of the other ambassadors. She could see them as they saw themselves, if she wanted to. And whenever she did that, she always compared their alien appearance to familiar sorts of animals: *That one looks like a flying bear. This one looks like a wolf-fish—or a wolf-mermaid. A fish bitten by a werewolf, maybe.* The other ambassadors never *really* looked like the animals she compared them to; they looked like themselves, and utterly alien to her. Nadia's brain would just try to fit new shapes into old words, because brains like to do that.

The Khelone really did look like turtles, though—or else like tortoises, the kind with long legs and very long necks.

Nadia lifted her helmet visor. The Khelone's helmet folded back inside its suit to reveal large eyes and a turtle-like beak.

"Translation ready?" Nadia whispered.

The Envoy pushed the lumpy translation node toward them. Pale lights flashed and flickered in the center of it.

Nadia's surroundings shifted. She no longer saw the inside of the Zvezda station pod. Instead she saw mountains. Footage from the fake window screen leaked out of its frame to surround her. The view looked grainy, awkward, and false. It gave her a headache.

"Can you turn down the scenery?" she whispered.

The Envoy made adjustments. The grainy mountain landscape flickered and faded away. Then the Khelone changed shape to become human-looking. He wore a brown leather jacket and an aviator's scarf, like a kid dressed up as a biplane pilot. He also looked like a young Yuri Gagarin—the very first cosmonaut.

Nadia did not approve. Everyone she knew in school had had a huge crush on Yuri Gagarin. The whole Soviet Union had had a huge crush on Yuri Gagarin. And Nadia had squeezed her aunt's hand while filing by Yuri Gagarin's coffin at the grand state funeral. It felt wrong in every way to see an illusory version of him now.

She concentrated hard and tried to change how the Khelone looked to her, but it didn't work. Nadia had never been good at manipulating her own translated perceptions. She wasn't any good at fooling herself.

The Envoy scootched off to the side and shifted between several uncomfortable shades of purple. It didn't like being there. Its purpose was to choose and guide ambassadors, not to participate in diplomatic conversations. Nadia was responsible for the actual talking.

"Hello," she said to her invited guest, voice carefully formal and respectful. "I am Nadia Antonovna Kollontai, ambassador of Terra and all Terran life." (The word *Earth* always sounded more official in Latin.)

"Hi," he answered, his voice neither respectful nor formal. He grinned with Yuri's wide grin. "I'm Remscalan of the Khelone Clusters. Call me Rem."

"Welcome," Nadia said, a little wary now.

"Thanks." Rem looked around. Nadia wondered what he saw, exactly. She wondered what the makeshift visual translation looked like to him. He used to be an ambassador himself, when he was still a Khelone kid and not yet an adolescent pilot, so the translator should work well for him—but it was a clumsy sort of translation compared to the Embassy. "I'm amazed you're alive out here," he said. "This is a bare-bones tent you've pitched."

Nadia bristled. She tried not to. Hadn't she just called Zvezda the rusting edge of Soviet technology in the privacy of her own head? But she lived here, and her own family had helped to design this place, throw it through the void, and build it on the moon. She had every right to mock her own home. The Khelone didn't.

"We're only just learning how to leave the planet," she said, her voice barely diplomatic. "It wasn't easy to arrange the neutral meeting place that you needed."

Rem gave her a long look, and then held up both hands. "Khelone ships can't land on planets as large as yours. Well, we *can*, but we'd never be able to take off again afterward. Escape velocity is difficult for those of us who've never had to bother with planets at all. And getting stuck planetside wouldn't be useful. You did call me here for transportation, right? You gave our new ambassador rare maps in exchange for a ride."

Nadia had pieced together maps and information from the Seventh Fiefdom, the Volen Enclaves, and the People of the Domes. Those maps were all rare because the Outlast had since swallowed the Seventh Fiefdom, the Volen Enclaves, and the People of the Domes. Those three civilizations were now extinct.

"I've heard you can travel fast," she said. "That you're good at taking *shortcuts*."

Rem rested both hands behind his head. "True. I made it here almost instantly."

I sent you a message more than a year ago, Nadia thought, but didn't say. Time flows differently when you move fast.

"Excellent," she said aloud. "Then I need you to accomplish a momentous and probably impossible feat of piloting skill."

"I'm interested," Rem said, and smiled wider.

The silly leather jacket and aviator scarf is a good translation, Nadia thought. *He really is that sort of pilot. He's delighted to try some new and dangerous thing.*

"We are going to fly into the Machinae lanes," she said.

Rem gave her a sideways look. "I think your translation node just broke. I definitely heard the wrong preposition."

"We're going inside the lanes," Nadia said again.

He shook his head. "Are you joking? I can't tell if you're joking. No one goes into the lanes, silly human. We skip across the surface instead. We can sidestep light speed by riding in the Machinae's wake, skimming right across those rippling waves of warped space-time. *Barnacle* and I are better at that kind of wake-hopping than anyone—"

Nadia tried not to laugh. The ship's name probably sounded more dignified than *Barnacle* in Rem's own language.

"—We can fly close to the lanes and their scrambled sense of gravity more skillfully than anyone else you could possibly find. But no one ever flies *into* the lanes."

"Untrue," Nadia said. "Witnesses tell me otherwise. The astronomers of the Seventh Fiefdom saw ships emerge from inside the lanes. So did the People of the Domes. Cartographers of the Volen Enclaves heard it happen while making their song-maps."

Rem looked serious now. His posture lost its casual, adolescent unconcern. "I hear bad things about the Fiefdom, Domes, and Enclaves. What happened to them *after* they saw ships fly from the lanes?"

"They all died," Nadia told him.

In her memory she heard heavy boots outside a cupboard door, though she tried very hard not to.

"You used to represent the Khelone," she went on. "Honor the trade I negotiated with the ambassador who took your place."

And you're curious, she added, just to herself. *Now that you're starting to think this is possible, you really want to try it. I can tell. Even through the fuzzy translation, I can still tell.*

Rem tossed the end of his aviator scarf over one shoulder in a cartoonishly rakish way.

"Fine," he said. "Come aboard. Are you ready to leave?"

Nadia nodded. "I will be in just a moment."

The Khelone stepped aside and turned away, waiting. The Envoy scootched closer to Nadia. "You did well," it whispered.

"I suppose," said Nadia—which was her way of saying "Yes, I know I did."

"It's good that you didn't share much more about your intentions," the Envoy added. "The pilot will be less likely to make this venture if the trip seems entirely futile."

Nadia laughed. The Envoy sounded even more like her uncle whenever it said something so pessimistic. "Do *you* think this is futile? It's a little late to say so, if you do."

The Envoy held its puppetlike mouth at a low, despondent angle. "No," it said. "I hope not. But your post is here. Your world needs its ambassador."

Nadia reached over and gently poked the Envoy's nose with a fingertip. It didn't actually have a nose, but she poked its purple translucent skin just above the sock-puppet shape of its mouth. She wanted to offer a hug, but the smooshy Envoy didn't hug very well.

"Go home," she said. "Don't wait around for me to come back. No telling how long that'll take. Use the return capsule and go choose a new ambassador."

The Envoy gave a slow and heavy nod. "The capsule

was damaged when we first launched, but I should be able to repair it."

"Be careful landing," Nadia warned. "Those things don't land very well. They just ram into the planet."

"Then I'll try to aim for an ocean," the Envoy said. "I might even select a whale as your successor. Whales are less impulsive than humans, and aquatic mammals already know what it's like to belong to more than one sort of world."

"Sounds good," Nadia said. "Choose a whale. Choose whoever and whatever you like—except Vanechka Vladimirovna. If you end up back in Moscow I absolutely forbid you to choose her."

"Your classmate is both charming and harmless," the Envoy said.

Nadia knew that the Envoy was just trying to annoy her. It worked. "She's neither. She's willfully ignorant. She thinks Father Frost is real and not just someone's drunk grandfather mixing up all the New Year's presents. She thinks you can get pregnant by holding hands."

"Some species probably can," the Envoy said thoughtfully. "Life enjoys infinite variety in infinite combinations."

"Then you may browse the magnificent variety of

life on Earth to pick whatever ambassador you see fit. Choose a whale. Choose a squid. Choose a beetle. But do not choose Vanechka Vladimirovna."

"Very well, Ambassador. I can promise you that much."

"Good-bye, Envoy."

"Good-bye, Nadia."

She hooked up a new breathing unit to her bulky orange suit. She wouldn't need much oxygen to cross over to the Khelone ship, and the air inside *Barnacle* was supposed to be breathable, but she still intended to travel with a full tank and a spare tank.

Rem stepped back inside the translation matrix, clearly impatient. "Ready?"

"Just about," Nadia told him. She grabbed a duffel bag already stocked full of food, water, spare clothes, a spare ventilation unit, and a notebook. Luckily, it didn't weigh nearly as much as it would have on Earth.

"Good," said Rem. He poked the module wall with one gloved finger. "This bare-bones tent of yours makes me nervous. I expect it to collapse at any moment."

"This is my home," Nadia said, with just a touch of warning in her voice. "I'm the first member of my species to live off-world. That's no small accomplishment, however bare-bones the tent."

"I meant no offense," Rem said—though he clearly

enjoyed causing offense. "But what you say isn't actually true."

"Excuse me?" Nadia asked, her tone extremely diplomatic. "Which part?"

"You aren't the first member of your species to live off-world. Not even close."

He walked away from the translation matrix and turned back into a turtle before Nadia could respond.

3

Zvezda Lunar Base: Present Day

Gabriel Sandro Fuentes, the ambassador of his world, was not on his world. He stood on the moon, inside the abandoned Zvezda base, face-to-face with an alien ambassador who looked far less alien than he had expected.

"You're human," he said. "How can you be human?"

Ambassador Kaen answered in a language that Gabe did not understand.

The two of them stared at each other, tense and wary, still unsure how much they could trust their new and fragile truce.

The Kaen fleet is an ancient, nomadic, and absolutely alien civilization of migratory starships, Gabe thought. *How can they have a human ambassador? We haven't ever traveled farther away than the moon, this moon, the one we're both standing on.*

He took in a deep breath of stale, Zvezda-processed air and let it out slowly. Ambassadors usually met in the Embassy, in the very center of the galaxy, where all of their languages and perceptions filtered through universal translation. They usually understood each other.

"Envoy?" Gabe called out. "Help?"

The Envoy scootched around the floor, reached out with a purple, puppetlike limb, and fiddled with old equipment.

"Just a moment." It sounded almost exactly like Gabe's mother when it spoke. Almost. "Let me dust off this old translator. Just a moment . . ."

Gabe made eye contact with Kaen, tapped his ear, and then pointed at the mess of machinery the Envoy was fiddling with. Kaen seemed to understand. She folded her hands, looked away, and waited.

He tried not to stare at her. Most human cultures considered staring rude, challenging, and aggressive. Most mammal species on Earth seemed to feel the same way about prolonged eye contact. And Gabe had worked hard to avoid aggression between them. They had a truce. They had a deal. Neither one of them was currently trying to get the other killed. So he tried not to stare.

This wasn't easy. He took in a sideways glance and then looked away.

The other ambassador wore a green space suit, jade-colored. The helmet of her suit looked very much like the headgear of Olmec statues, carved in ancient Mexico long before the Spanish came conquering across the ocean, before even the Aztecs came conquering southward from North America. Gabe's family had kitschy salt and pepper shakers carved into the very same shape at home—or at least they used to, when they still had a home, before the house was swallowed by a small black hole in the Kaen's first attempt to assassinate him.

Gabe tried not to dwell on that.

The Olmec heads look like astronauts, he had once said of the salt and pepper shakers.

His mom had absolutely hated that idea. *They're ball players,* she'd insisted. *Ancient ball players wearing football helmets. It would hurt to get hit in the head with a great big lump of solid rubber. They are definitely, definitely not astronauts.*

Gabe wondered how to explain his current absence to his mother. *I'm so sorry that I had to disappear on the very same day Dad got deported. The timing alone probably broke your heart and stomped on the pieces. But I had to go to the moon. . . .*

Gabe tried not to think about either one of his parents. He risked another sideways glance at the Kaen ambassador.

She looks a bit tense, he thought. *Not tense as in anxious, but tense like a guitar string, or a bow string—or maybe a string stretched between two tin cans to make a telephone. I wonder if I look just as tense. Probably.*

"There!" the Envoy said. "That should do it. Say something."

Gabe didn't notice any difference. He had expected to feel something when the translation matrix turned on, something like the mild headache he always got, right in the middle of his forehead, whenever someone spoke Spanish faster than he could follow.

He turned to Kaen. "Ambassador?"

"Ambassador," she answered, voice equally formal and now understandable.

How are you human? Gabe wanted to demand, again. He wanted to shout that question. *How can you possibly be human?* But he swallowed his inner shouting. It wouldn't be diplomatic to start their conversation with demands.

"Thanks for coming in person," he said. "Thank you for showing so much trust."

"I trust our truce more easily than I trust this place," she said, looking around. "The walls don't look very stable."

"No, they really don't," Gabe agreed.

The Envoy quietly grumbled in the corner. Gabe caught the words "triumph of engineering," but little else.

"We should leave," Gabe went on. "I can point out where we're headed when we get closer to the planet, once I can see the shapes of the different continents. Hopefully there won't be too much cloud cover."

"That won't be a problem," Kaen said. "We aren't going down to the planet."

"Excuse me?" Gabe asked.

"We will not be traveling to the homeworld at this time," she said, slowly and carefully. She looked down at the makeshift translator with obvious skepticism.

"*Excuse* me?" Gabe asked again. Then he took a breath and adjusted his tone. "That was a condition of our truce. We negotiated this already. I need passage back to the planet. Earth. Terra. Home. The one right over there."

"We did not speak of timing," she said. "I intend to bring you back to the planet's surface. But not immediately. I must return directly to the fleet, and I . . . invite you to come with me. The captains insist on a meeting."

"The ones who ordered my assassination." Gabe knew he probably shouldn't bring up conflicts that the two of them had already resolved, but he did anyway.

"Yes," she agreed, without embarrassment or apology.

Gabe felt something close to panic. "I have urgent business at home," he tried to explain. *Mostly because I don't have a home. It imploded. Then it burned. And then Dad got kicked out of the country because of a stop sign. Now my sister Lupe is going to split her time between babysitting and summer school, and she hates both, and her hair is probably catching fire every single time she talks to Mom, and I'm not there. I need to be there. Dad needs to be there. I need to find him.*

"You have more urgent business in the fleet," Kaen said, unruffled. She lifted her helmet. "So do I. Please hurry. I assume you have some kind of suit."

"I don't actually know," Gabe admitted. "Envoy? Are there any spare suits around here?"

"Yes," the Envoy said. "Twenty years ago I did tear up one of the suits to patch wall leaks, but the other spare should still be serviceable. It might even fit you. Most cosmonauts were small of stature in order to squeeze into very small capsules."

Gabe still felt close to panic. He couldn't stop that feeling, but he could set it aside. "Just a moment, then. I'll suit up."

Ambassador Kaen waited by the front airlock while Gabe and the Envoy went looking for the spare suit.

"Envoy?" Gabe whispered.

"You don't need to keep your voice down," the Envoy told him. "We're outside the translation matrix now. Your colleague can't understand us."

"My colleague is human," said Gabe.

"I also noticed this, yes."

"How? How is that possible? We haven't traveled any farther than the moon. Right here."

"You haven't traveled farther in ships of your own making," said the Envoy. "But some of your species may have hitched a ride on other ships, made by other civilizations. The Kaen fleet might well have passed through this system long ago. Many different species travel with them, and all consider themselves equally Kaen. Yours seem to be among them."

"Don't you *remember* a Kaen visit?" Gabe asked. "Aren't you extremely old?"

"Memory is vague and uncertain over long stretches of time," the Envoy admitted.

They found an orange, empty cosmonaut suit hanging on a wall. The letters cccp had been stenciled across the white helmet.

"What does that stand for?" Gabe asked, pointing.

"Союз Советских Социалистических Республик," said the Envoy. "It is the Cyrillic abbreviation for the USSR."

"Oh." The suit looked creepy, like a suit of armor in

a haunted castle. Gabe wondered if any of his father's emergency ghost plans would work on a moon base. Several of those stories involved wailing and unquiet spirits who wandered near bodies of water and tried to drown anybody who got too close. Maybe dying in a vacuum felt like drowning. Probably not. And Gabe didn't know of any NASA astronauts who had died all the way out here—though the ones on Apollo 13 almost did. Maybe some secret Russian mission had gone badly and left ghost-cosmonauts behind. Maybe they wandered like La Llorona and tried to share the experience of vacuum death with everyone they met.

"What are thinking of, Ambassador?" the Envoy asked.

"I'm wondering if Zvezda is haunted," said Gabe. "I don't really believe in ghosts, but I'm wondering anyway."

"Zvezda is haunted by frustrated possibilities," the Envoy said. "It is haunted by a vision of the future that never happened, by planned lunar cities that were never built. And for forty years it was haunted by me."

Gabe took the suit down off the wall and tried to figure out how to put it on. The Envoy tried to help. This took a while.

"Are you confident in your truce with the Kaen?" the Envoy asked while struggling with glove clasps. "And are you sure of this course of action?"

"I don't see much choice," Gabe said.

The Envoy shook its puppetlike head. "There are always choices. The options currently available to you aren't ideal, but they do exist—and you do seem to be making the best choices under the circumstances. Traveling to the Kaen fleet, even as a kind of prisoner, is preferable to death by drill cannon. I also agree that it's preferable to ineffectual abandonment here. I would rather not repeat *that* experience. But I don't know what transpired between you and Ambassador Kaen at the Embassy, and I don't understand why the Kaen would try to harm you in the first place."

"They were scared," Gabe explained. "They're hiding, and they hate that. They hate to hold still. Kaen thought I would reveal their position—which *was* our plan, pretty much, when we thought they were just pirates."

"Aren't they?" the Envoy asked.

"No," Gabe said. "They're refugees. So I came up with a new plan."

"It seems to have worked," the Envoy said.

"So far." Gabe fiddled with the mechanism of his helmet visor. Then he paused. "Is there anything to eat around here? I'm kind of hungry. It's been a long time since those granola bars in the park."

The Envoy scooted across the station module, checked

a few storage containers, and came back with a metal toothpaste tube.

"What's this?" Gabe asked. He couldn't read the Russian label.

"Borscht," the Envoy said. "Beet soup. That's what the label says, though Ambassador Nadia refused to call it borscht."

Gabe felt extremely skeptical about eating borscht from a toothpaste tube. "How does it taste?"

"Nadia described it as a mixture of apathy and pain."

"Right, then." He removed the cap, took a breath, and squeezed the dark substance into his mouth. "Yep," he said, once he was sure he could keep the stuff down. "Accurate description."

"I can only hope that our hosts will feed you better," the Envoy said. "Given that humans travel with the Kaen, some of their food should be edible to you."

"Here's hoping." Gabe tossed the empty tube back into the storage container. "Okay. Here we go."

Ambassador Kaen led the way to the shuttle, which crouched on lunar stone like a carved jaguar.

Three mining craft flanked the shuttle. They skittered like massive silverfish, and kept the single eye of their drill cannons pointed at Gabe. He tried not to pay them any attention, but it was difficult to pay attention to anything else. He stumbled and almost dropped the Envoy.

Careful, the Envoy wrote across its surface in glowing purple letters. It had condensed into a small and solid sphere. Gabe held it cradled in his right arm. He carried his backpack, his great-grandfather's cane sword, and the suit's oxygen tank with his left. This was difficult, not because the stuff was heavy—none of it weighed very much on the moon—but because it was awkwardly shaped, and because the sleeves of his space suit were awkwardly bulky.

"Sorry," Gabe said, even though the word stayed inside his helmet. The Envoy couldn't possibly hear him.

He glanced up. Stars burned above in every color. Then he stumbled again and tried to watch where he was going in the dim light cast by the Kaen ships.

The jaguar-shaped shuttlecraft opened its mouth. The two ambassadors climbed inside to be swallowed by it.

4

The inside of the shuttlecraft looked spare and utilitarian. Most of the surfaces were metallic, either chrome or dark green. The back wall was made of something softer, with human-shaped indentations. It looked like someone had pressed action figures into a flattened lump of greenish Play-Doh.

Kaen crossed the floor to stand against one of the depressions in the wall. She waved at Gabe to do the same.

The shuttle closed its mouth and shifted positions to face upward, away from the moon. The back wall became the floor. The Envoy rolled away from Gabe. Then it poked his arm and pointed at his cane.

Oh, right, Gabe thought. *This could be a dangerous, suit-puncturing thing during launch.* He pushed both cane sword and backpack off to the side. Then he looked at

Kaen. She held up one hand, extended all five fingers, and started a countdown. *Five. Four. Three. Two. One. Closed fist. Zero. Liftoff.*

Acceleration pushed the passengers down as the shuttle climbed upward. Then both the shuttle and everything inside it moved at the same speed, and the words *down* and *up* ceased to mean anything. Gabe floated weightless.

Kaen opened the front of her helmet. Gabe tried to do the same, but it took him a while to work the clasp with his suit gloves on, and he wasn't really sure how to take the suit gloves off.

"We have translation here," Kaen told him once he finally lifted his helmet visor. "Most of our ships do. Many different species are Kaen, and no mouth among us is shaped to speak all languages, so we need translators often. As an ambassador you may also see flickers of visual translation. People who are not human may flicker in and out of human shapes."

Gabe finally asked what his brain burned to ask. "How long have humans traveled with the Kaen?"

"Thousands of years," she said. "Probably. Time moves differently when you travel at different speeds, so I couldn't tell you how many times your homeworld circled the sun since we left."

"It's your homeworld too," Gabe pointed out.

"No, it isn't." Her words were solid, fixed, and inarguable. "I am Kaen. I speak for the Kaen. We move between stars. No single system is ever home to us. Our homeworld is the fleet."

Her tone of voice convinced Gabe to set aside all other questions about shared origins, no matter how badly they demanded to be asked.

"How long will it take us to reach the fleet from here?" he asked instead. "And who is piloting?"

"Not very long," said Kaen. "And I am. Try not to distract me too much."

"Sorry." Gabe looked around. "There aren't any windows. How can you see outside?"

Kaen tapped her fingers against the forearm of her suit instead of answering.

A glowing projection of the space outside took shape inside the shuttle.

Gabe looked behind them to see the sun retreating. Both Earth and the moon had already disappeared in the distance. All three of the mining craft followed close behind the shuttle. Watching them felt like making eye contact. Gabe looked away. He looked ahead. Mars grew larger as they approached.

"Did you build any pyramids on Mars before you left our solar system?" Gabe asked. He couldn't help asking.

Kaen creased up her forehead. "Which one is Mars?"

"There," Gabe said. "The fourth one out from the sun. We're flying directly at it."

"Not directly," said Kaen. "We'll slingshot around it to gain momentum. And no, I don't think we built any pyramids. The Kaen don't ever build planetside. We build ships. We travel. If there are pyramids on Mars then someone else made them."

"There aren't really," Gabe said, feeling sheepish. "But some of the mountains look like pyramids when we see them through telescopes. Sort of. If you squint."

"What do they look like from the surface?" Kaen asked.

"We haven't been to the surface," Gabe admitted.

Kaen nodded. "I remember that now. Your civilization hasn't traveled farther than the moon we just left."

"We did send robots to Mars," Gabe said. He tried not to sound defensive, but he did anyway.

"That would be easier," said Kaen.

Gabe wanted to explain how unspeakably cool the *Curiosity* rover was, but he didn't. Kaen tapped the controls on her forearm again. She looked intent. He tried not to be distracting. He watched the projected image of Mars, which took up most of the shuttle interior. He also thought about his mom.

* * * *

"There were no ancient astronauts," she had always insisted.

"Why not?" Gabe had asked her, once and only once. "I still think those Olmec helmets look like space suits."

Lupe shook her head and tried to shush him. She knew that the question would provoke a rant from their mother. But Gabe didn't know that, not yet, and he noticed the shushing too late. Then Lupe upended the helmeted saltshaker to pour a whole mess of the stuff over her dinner. This made Dad irate. He grumbled, "You're wrecking an ideal balance of spice and flavor, you salt addict." But he did not grumble more loudly than Mom.

"Why would aliens go around teaching people how to make pyramids?" she asked. She had a warning edge to her voice, something that Gabe would later recognize as an incoming Teachable Moment.

"The alien ship needed a pyramid to land on in the *Stargate* movie," he said. "That could be one reason why."

Mom carefully set her fork down on the table. "Listen to me, my heart."

"Or maybe aliens might have—"

"Listen to me."

Gabe listened.

Mom made eye contact and held it. "To give *aliens*

credit for our ancient, prehistoric accomplishments in astronomy, or mathematics, or pyramid building, is to deny *us* those accomplishments. Please don't ever suggest that aliens flew down to teach the Olmec their business."

"Okay," said Gabe.

Mom smiled a warm smile and picked up her fork.

Something else bothered Gabe about finding humans among the Kaen, something more than his mother's objections to quack anthropology and its weird obsessions with pyramid-building aliens.

We were just getting started, he thought. *We're only just learning how to leave the nest, and that's horrifying and wonderful and we don't know how any of it works, yet, but we're going to find out. We put a robot on Mars with a crazy sky crane. Dad and I stayed up really late to watch it happen, and every time the control room got a signal from* Curiosity *they called it a "heartbeat," and everyone cheered when it landed. Dad and I cheered. We almost woke up the twins. NASA engineers were crying and jumping up and down in the middle of the night. We're learning how to do this. We're figuring it out . . . but now it looks like we already did. Humans already live in deep space. We hoped that would happen someday, but it already happened and we missed it.*

He watched Mars as the shuttle shot around it. He watched as they left it behind.

"We're in the asteroid belt now," Kaen told him.

"Really?" Gabe looked around, but saw no asteroids. He thought this part of their trip would involve exciting duck-and-weave maneuvers between huge rocks, but the asteroids were spaced farther apart than he had expected.

"Really," Kaen said. "This is our destination up ahead. The largest asteroid."

"Ceres," Gabe said automatically. He was the kind of kid who knew such things.

"It's a useful place," Kaen said. "Plenty of ice on the surface." Then she looked embarrassed. Resource theft from an inhabited system was a serious offense, and the Kaen had not asked for permission before mining the ice. But they hadn't been able to. This system had lacked an ambassador for forty years after Nadia Antonovna Kollontai left the post.

"If you need the ice, then you're welcome to it," Gabe said. "I told you that already." Nomads know how important it is to share water in the desert.

Kaen nodded in acknowledgment and thanks. "Float near the back wall," she said. "I need to turn the craft around to slow down."

Gabe pushed off with his fingertips. He passed right

through the projection of Ceres to reach the squishy wall.

The Envoy took in a breath, let it out like a leaky balloon, and propelled itself through the shuttle. It caught up Gabe's floating backpack and cane on its way.

Kaen followed. Then she held up one hand and extended her fingers for another countdown. *Five. Four. Three. Two. One. Fist.*

The shuttle fired its engines. This slowed down the ship itself, but everyone inside it was pushed by their own momentum into the wall. Gabe felt extremely heavy for one long moment. He squeezed his eyes shut.

The extra weight eased. Gabe opened his eyes. The projection of Ceres now filled up his view completely. Sunlight flashed and glinted from it, reflected by the frozen ocean that covered the whole surface of the asteroid. They dove down at it directly.

The Envoy cleared its throat in a nervous way. "We're coming in fast for a landing."

"We're not landing," Kaen said. She tapped forearm controls in a calm and deliberate way.

The frozen ocean no longer looked smooth. Mountains, valleys, and craters appeared in the projected view. Kaen held up one arm and gestured. The movement of the ship followed the movement of her hand and it nose-dived into one of the craters.

Gabe felt like he was on a roller coaster. He hated roller coasters. He clenched every single muscle he had and braced for a crash. But this crater was deep. It kept going, down and farther down. It opened into a massive cave inside the ice.

Lights clustered together in that cavernous space. At first they looked like distant stars. Then they looked like fireflies blinking out messages and circling each other.

The shuttlecraft flew closer, flew in among the flashing lights. Gabe saw that they were starships.

Vessels of all different shapes, sizes, and designs moved together. Some looked like flying mountains or interlocking rings. Others zipped and flitted like minnows among leviathans.

"We welcome you to the fleet, Ambassador," Kaen said, her voice low.

"Thank you, Ambassador," Gabe said. "This does look like a good place to hide."

Kaen's voice turned bitter. "This is a good place to be utterly trapped. One exit, easily blocked. Not ideal."

Gabe had nothing to say to that. He watched the different ships go by in their projected view. Then he laughed, delighted.

"What's funny?" Kaen asked.

"That one," he said. "The silver flying saucer up ahead.

Back home people usually imagine that alien ships look just like that. I'm laughing because they were right. There really are flying saucers. I think that's funny."

Kaen gave him an odd look. "I also find this funny, but for different reasons. That's not an alien ship. That is *our* ship."

5

Gabe stared at the flying saucer, the kind of ship that humans had long imagined slicing through space like a flat stone skipped over a pond surface—the kind of ship that other humans apparently lived in.

"Really?" he asked.

"Really," Kaen said.

"That's fantastic," Gabe said.

"I'm glad you think so," said Kaen. If she was *actually* glad, Gabe couldn't hear it in the tone of her translated voice. The Kaen ambassador was not effusive.

She held up one hand and guided the shuttlecraft closer.

"It looks like a calendar," Gabe whispered. "Up close. The markings on top of the saucer look like an old stone calendar."

"The name of our ship is the *Calendar*," Kaen told him.

Gabe felt the shuttlecraft shudder as they docked at the very edge of the saucer rim. The squishy wall behind them became a squishy floor beneath them. Gabe stood up. *The saucer must be spinning,* he thought. *That pushes us out and away from the center.*

Kaen pressed her hand against the wall that used to be the floor. A ladder appeared, leading up to the shuttle entrance. She pointed at Gabe's helmet. "Close your suit. The airlock will be empty on the other side."

The Envoy hardened itself into a bowling ball so the vacuum wouldn't hurt.

Kaen climbed the ladder.

Gabe sealed up his helmet visor. He slung his backpack over one shoulder, hoisted the solid and spherical Envoy under his left arm, took up the cane and ventilation unit in his left hand, and then used his free hand to climb after Kaen.

The shuttle door opened above them. They climbed up into the airlock, where one of the walls suddenly became the floor. Gabe almost made a face-plant against it. Kaen stepped smoothly onto the new floor as their sense of down shifted.

The door behind them closed. Another door opened ahead. Gabe and the Envoy followed Kaen through the passage, where gravity gradually increased to a full

Terran-G. Gabe discovered that his suit was heavy—especially the oxygen tank, which he had to carry like a bulky suitcase.

They don't make this *gravity by spinning,* he thought as he struggled. *The rim of the saucer is behind us now, and we're not getting pushed out that way.*

Doors opened and closed automatically as they approached. Each doorway was much wider at the base, like a triangle with the topmost point cut off.

The passageway led to a small, square room with walls that looked like the inside of a warehouse, or the hull of a ship, or the frame of a submarine. Struts and supports all stood visible. A woven mat dyed blue and yellow stretched across the floor, and that was the only decoration.

Four glowing lamps hung from the ceiling on thin cables. They looked like bioluminescent jellyfish, or like any other deep-sea creature that knew how to make its own light. Gabe couldn't see any jellyfish swimming around inside the lamp. He guessed that much smaller creatures were glowing in there. Bacteria, maybe.

Kaen knelt on the woven mat. Gabe followed her lead and sat beside her. He set his pack and cane in front of him. The Envoy scootched over to settle on Gabe's other side.

They waited.

Gabe's nose itched, but he didn't know if it was safe to lift his helmet visor—and with the helmet sealed he had no way to ask Kaen. Even if he could lift the helmet, breathe, and ask a question, he didn't even know if this room had a translation matrix turned on yet, so he waited and tried not to think about the unreachable itching of his nose.

The metal door opened. Two tall figures came through it. Both were human, male, and dressed in pale gray. Complex and unfamiliar patterns covered the fabric of their clothes. They had long, straight hair slicked back to show high foreheads. Neither one of them looked at or acknowledged the ambassadors. Instead they stood to either side of the open doorway in classic guard pose, shoulders squared—but they carried covered trays instead of weapons. Unless the covered trays *were* weapons. The two did look strong and serious enough to wield a tray in deadly fashion.

Kaen's helmet retracted. The segments collapsed and slid behind the shoulders of her suit. Gabe took that as a signal and lifted his own visor. The ship's air smelled metallic and clean.

No one moved. Everyone continued to wait. The door remained open. Gabe scratched his nose.

A thin and spidery woman joined them through the

open door. She had white hair cut very short, an ornate necklace of small blue stones, and dark skin creased by a thousand wrinkles.

"Hello, little mouths," the woman said. Gabe heard the words in very heavily accented English.

Kaen sat up straighter. "Great Speaker," she said, her voice *extra* formal, obviously annoyed, and trying hard not to be. "I present the ambassador of our host system, one who offers us guest gifts."

Host system, Gabe thought. *She called this their host system, a place they just happen to be passing through—a place they happen to be hiding in. This system is just another rest stop. They don't think of it as home.*

The Great Speaker looked down at Gabe as though unsure of his species.

"Astonishing," she said. "These offered guest gifts come soon after we wore snake blood."

Gabe blinked. He understood the words, but not how they fit together.

"We found a more diplomatic solution," Kaen said.

That made sense to him, at least.

The Great Speaker knelt on the other side of the woven mat, but she kept her voice aloof. "I am Nicanmorohua Cihuatlatoani. I say so. I, the Speaker. And here aboard this ship, among the Kaen, I serve as Great Speaker and captain. Address me as Speaker Tlatoani when you yourself speak, little mouth."

Gabe understood Kaen's annoyance now. *She's treating us like children. We are children, sure, but we're also ambassadors.*

He tapped into his father's goofy love of high formality—though hopefully without the goofiness.

"Great Speaker," Gabe said. "I am Ambassador Gabriel Sandro Fuentes of Terra. I am honored by your welcome. But you may not address me as 'little mouth.'"

The Speaker gave him a long and intense look. In that moment she reminded Gabe of the old woman in the city park near his house—the one who sat and watched children as though planning to eat them.

"She calls *everyone* 'little mouth,'" Kaen whispered. "*Mouth* just means 'person.' Though it *also* means 'mouth.'"

"Why doesn't it translate as 'person,' then?" Gabe asked.

"Because adults don't ever translate well. Their words and ideas become weirdly literal in translation."

Gabe nodded. That made perfect sense to him.

The Speaker took a knife from her robe, thin-bladed and clear as though made out of glass.

The Envoy made an unhappy noise.

Gabe stared at the knife. He reached for his sword-cane, and then pulled his hand back. "Ambassador Kaen?

Does your captain still want to assassinate me, or is this a challenge to some kind of duel?"

Kaen shook her head, but she didn't offer any further help or explanation.

The Speaker looked amused. "This knife is not an invitation to contest or combat. But you may carry terrible invasions with you. Our welcome requires your blood."

That was not reassuring.

Your space suits look like Olmec statue helmets, Gabe thought. *Your shuttlecraft crouches like a jade jaguar. And now we're talking about blood sacrifices?*

"I didn't come here to invade," he said, aloud and carefully. "I was invited. And I know that I must look very intimidating—an eleven-year-old kid stuffed into a forty-year-old cosmonaut suit—but I promise you that I have no plans to conquer the Kaen."

I really shouldn't be joking, he thought with instant regret. *Jokes don't translate well, not at all. And I shouldn't have pointed out the already obvious fact that I'm just a kid. She doesn't respect us enough as it is.*

He was relieved when the Speaker laughed. She did seem to be laughing with him rather than laughing at him.

"She needs a blood *sample,*" Kaen explained. "She's worried about invasions of disease."

The Speaker nodded. "We must know if you carry strange plagues that could wreak gleeful havoc on our bodies here. I will not welcome you aboard my ship until I have your blood to analyze."

"Oh," said Gabe. "I understand now. You're worried about smallpox."

"What's smallpox?" Kaen asked.

"Something our mutual ancestors had no defense against. Okay, then." Gabe unsealed his gloves and held out one bare hand.

Speaker Tlatoani took the hand, not roughly but not gently either. She held the knife up to Gabe's palm and pricked the skin with the very tip. It was sharp. Gabe couldn't even feel the cut at first. Then he felt it, and winced.

The Speaker pressed her knife against the cut. Blood seeped into the hollow core, turning the clear blade red. She took the knife away and slapped a small, sticky patch of cloth over the tiny wound. Gabe felt it burn. Then it itched. Then it tickled in a very slight and irritating way, and after that it didn't feel like anything.

Meanwhile the Speaker stood, pushed the blade into a wall panel, and twisted the hilt. "Now we wait to unfold your blood stories." She waved one hand at the guards. Both stepped forward to set trays in front of Gabe and Kaen. "Eat while we wait."

Kaen took the cover off of hers. Gabe did the same. Each tray held four small cakes made out of cornmeal.

"This is reciprocal protection for you," the Speaker explained. "The tamales carry vaccines against germs that your body will meet here among us."

Kaen ate a cake. She didn't seem to savor it much.

"Thank you for the food and protection," Gabe said. He sniffed one of the cakes. It was definitely cornmeal, but dry and hardened rather than properly steamed. It still smelled better than tube borsht. His stomach gave a long, slow growl. Gabe took a bite and spent a long time chewing.

This is not a tamal, he thought. *This is nothing like a tamal. Dad would weep, and rage, and tear at his hair to hear these little corn cookies referred to as tamales. He'd call them* sordos, *without any kind of meat or fruit filling in the middle, and he would refuse to eat them. He would probably rather catch space smallpox than eat these.*

Gabe offered one to the Envoy, who quietly swallowed it. The cake remained visible inside its transparent, purple skin, slowly breaking apart. Gabe ate the other three. *Sorry, Dad. I'm hungry. And I don't want to catch any alien diseases.*

Noises chimed from the wall panel. The Speaker stood to examine the blood sample knife.

"Your blood tells no offensive stories," she reported. "Be welcome, then. You may come aboard. We wash our painted faces and set aside the blood of snakes." Her voice sounded less formal than the words she used. Gabe guessed that adult translation difficulties made her sound more ceremonial than she actually intended. "Now we will travel to the Library through Night and beneath Day. We must take counsel with other captains there."

6

Kaen dusted corn-cookie crumbs from her hands and stood, obviously impatient to be done with the airlock ceremonies. Gabe stood up more slowly.

"It'll take us a night and a day to get there?" he asked. "It took less time to get here from the moon."

"Night and Day are both *places*," Kaen explained. "Two cities in the middle of the ship. You'll understand better when you see them. And you can store your outersuit here if you don't want to carry it around. Looks heavy."

"It is," said Gabe, relieved. He fumbled with the complicated clasps and climbed out of the bulky cosmonaut suit. Then he put on his backpack and took up the walking cane. "Okay. Ready."

Speaker Tlatoani went elegantly through the passageways and led them into a much larger chamber. Crowds of people moved through it and flickered in and out of translation. Gabe tried not to stare at them. He was somewhat used to alien company, but he was not at all accustomed to seeing so many untranslated appearances directly, without a squint or a sideways glance.

The Speaker paused near a translation node. "This is the Avenue of the Dead, and we will ride through Night among them."

"Well, that sounds ominous," Gabe said. "This place looks more like a subway train station than the land of death."

"That's what she said," Kaen told him. "It just didn't translate well."

They moved on through the train station without calling any attention to themselves, but the crowd around them still parted for both their captain and their ambassador.

The subway train floated in place rather than running on wheels or tracks. It looked carved out of turquoise and jade, though the surface felt like lightweight metal rather than stone. There were no chairs inside. Handholds rose up from the floor, shaped to suit each occupant. Gabe heard very little conversational buzz, and he couldn't understand what he did hear.

"Envoy?" he said quietly.

"Yes?" the Envoy answered.

"I'm still not sure if we're honored guests or prisoners."

"These are not mutually exclusive categories, Ambassador."

"That's very comforting," Gabe said.

"I'm glad you feel comforted."

The train moved. It carried them silently away from the station, away from the saucer rim, and sped through tunnels toward the hub. Gabe watched the tunnel walls blur outside, hypnotic in the way that train rides always were. Then the train left the tunnel for the wide-open space of the saucer's interior.

Gabe saw Night and Day.

Each city stood above the other. Each one formed the other's sky.

He looked up. Tiny dots of people walked on the distant, day-lit ceiling. He looked down at the closer streets of Night. Lamps and windows burned with the same swirling phosphorescence as the smaller lanterns in the airlock welcoming room, and reflected light bounced down from the brighter city above to give its darker twin a dusky glow.

A stepped pyramid stood in the center of Night. A massive, bowl-shaped platform stood suspended at the apex of the pyramid. Sunlight burned inside the bowl, and shone upward at upside-down cornfields and the city of Day.

So they did build a space pyramid, Gabe thought, thrilled and almost laughing. *The temple of the sun. A very small sun. They built a pyramid for holding up the sun.*

The train moved through Night with rocket-like speed. Then it slowed, and Gabe caught a less blurry look at the view just outside his window. At first glance Night seemed like an ordinary urban place, built by humans to human proportions and human ways of moving around. It had buildings, streets, and crowds of people flowing like water unsure about which way was down.

I don't know which way is down, either, Gabe thought. He looked up at Day, and thought about the people of Day looking up at him.

At second glance the streets of Night looked utterly alien to Gabe. Most of the people were human, but not all. This was a Kaen city, and Kaen of other species moved through the streets. They flickered into human-seeming shapes when they passed translation nodes in public squares. Almost everyone wore thin clothing, brightly colored and easily seen in the dim light. Most walls were painted in equally bright colors.

Gabe wondered whether people spent half of their time in Day and the other half in Night, or else stayed mostly in one place or the other. He wondered if the streetlamps of Night looked like stars to the people in

Day, or if their miniature sun-in-a-bowl burned too brightly to see Night behind it. He wondered how their gravity worked.

The train entered a tunnel inside the base of the pyramid, cutting off his view. Then it slowed to a stop. Speaker Tlatoani disembarked. She didn't look back to make sure that the others followed her. The captain clearly expected to be followed.

Walls and ceilings inside the pyramid were covered with bright metal foil, all of it stamped in complex patterns and designs. Crowds of people moved and milled around or stood waiting for another train, just as they would at any other central station.

The Speaker led them to a very small room that was clearly an elevator. One wall displayed a cutaway map of the whole pyramid. Speaker Tlatoani touched the map and traced a route upward from where they were to where they were going. The doors closed. Gabe felt slightly heavier as the elevator moved.

"How does your gravity work?" he asked.

"It works very well," Tlatoani told him. "How did you enjoy your first sight of our home?" The Speaker was clearly proud and inviting Gabe to offer compliments.

"Amazing," he said, honestly.

"I am pleased that it amazed you," Tlatoani said. "We

built Night and Day according to the knowledge that time and space are not separate things. We built this ship and its cities to accommodate the needs of maize, and the needs of mouths, and the needs of the little sun we made. Even such a tiny sun must be the center of attention."

Kaen pointed at the etched pyramid map on the wall. "Our ambassador academy takes up this floor over here, and the command center of the ship is here, close to the sun."

"Is that where we're going?" Gabe asked.

"No," said the Speaker. "We will hold council with the other captains in the Library. Here." The elevator stopped. The doors opened. The Speaker held out one arm. "This is the home of our chronicles and codices, histories and discourses, high proverbs and tickling songs. This is the House of Painted Books."

The walls and floor of the library were made of dark and polished ceramic, which hid most of the space in warm shadows. Books sat on glowing podiums, waiting to be read, and the podiums themselves provided the primary source of light. The book pages were transparent with symbols printed in bright colors. Each page was bound at both ends, which made a single book into one long page folded up like an accordion. People stood reading in silence, their faces intent and lit from below. They looked like ghostly storytellers holding flashlights under their chins.

Speaker Tlatoani led the way to a separate chamber, one without shelves or podiums. A single, unfolded book lined the walls like a horizontal tapestry, every page of it visible at once.

Gabe read the translated writing: *Here is told how the people of maize and bonemeal and the blood of Quetzalcoatl came to travel nomadic between suns.*

The floor was a mosaic of small tiles, and also a map of a single planet. Gabe instantly recognized the shape of its continents.

A bright set of tiles marked central Mexico.

"This is the Chamber of the Homeworld," Speaker Tlatoani announced. "Here is told that history of several suns ago, and here we meet as a gesture of kinship. We who left to become Kaen were among the first city-makers. We were the best astronomers, and the very best mathematicians. The Kaen came visiting on their long migration and were impressed by our accomplishments, by our skills at math and stargazing, and by the play of our magnificent games. A sense of play is needful to establish communication."

"We know," Kaen said quietly. "We're ambassadors."

The Speaker went on as though Kaen hadn't said anything. "First the fleet offered trade in objects and stories, in the sorts of communication and cooperation that complex life and civilizations all depend on. Then they offered us membership within the fleet, and we accepted. Our oldest cities emptied into orbit to become Kaen."

Mom might not be so pissed about this after all, Gabe thought. *Aliens never built our pyramids. Aliens don't take the credit for ancient human accomplishments. They were impressed by what we had already accomplished.*

"Thank you for sharing this history, Speaker Tlatoani," Gabe said.

"None of it should be news to you," said the Speaker. "The homeworld should remember us. Your academy should hold and preserve the shape of such remembrance."

"They don't have an academy on the homeworld," said Kaen. She didn't say it in an insulting way, but Gabe still felt the sting of embarrassment at his lack of galactic education.

"This is astonishing," said the Speaker. "It also explains much."

The Envoy turned mortified shades of purple.

"Terrible things happened to each and every human academy I tried to build," it explained. "They burned in Tenochtitlán, and in Baghdad, and in Alexandria, and in the fires of Qin. Human academies do not last. Inhuman academies sometimes last longer. The descendants of elephant ambassadors maintained their mobile school for many generations, and they might well be teaching history and diplomacy to each other at this very moment. I hope so. But I don't know for sure. I have not selected an elephantine ambassador for some time."

"What's an elephant?" Kaen asked.

"A very big mammal," Gabe told her, relieved to be the one answering a question rather than asking it. "Large ears, prehensile trunks for noses. Migratory, like the Kaen. They're supposed to have very long memories, but I don't know if that's really true."

"It is," the Envoy said. "And their epic marching poems are very impressive."

The light inside the chamber dimmed.

"We will now take council with the other captains," said the Speaker.

"All of them?" Gabe asked. He had seen a great many Kaen ships outside, and he didn't think representatives of every ship would fit inside this room.

"No," said the Speaker. "Four captains will meet here,

two of them projected to join us remotely. We four take actions pertaining to snake blood and shields."

"Translation?" Gabe whispered to Kaen.

"They make emergency decisions," she told him, "especially those related to conflicts in general, and our evasion of the Outlast in particular."

Gabe understood what that meant. "These are the four captains who decided to kill me. Who turned my entanglement device into a house-swallowing black hole. Who sent ice-mining drones to shoot me down."

"Yes," said Kaen.

"Oh good." Gabe cracked his knuckles. "Should be a fun conversation, then."

Two glowing projections flickered and took shape inside the chamber. One of them had a beak, a large head crest, and long hair—though the hair looked more like anemones than anything hairy or feathery. Visual translation flickered on and off again. It transformed the projection into a male and humanlike figure, blond and frowning.

"Captain Qonne," the Speaker said as both a greeting and an introduction.

The other captain was a tree. Once translated, the tree looked androgynously human, and also like some sort of guru: seated, serene, and hovering above the floor.

"Captain Seiba," said the Speaker.

The fourth came physically into the chamber. He had to crouch down to pass through the doorway. This captain was tall, black-skinned, and potbellied. Untranslated he looked more like a massive metal suit. Mechanical arms and legs stuck out from the sides of a transparent sphere. An aquatic creature swam around in that sphere. The captain's potbelly was really a fishbowl.

"Captain Mumwat," said the Speaker. "Thanks to you all for joining us here."

"This the hatchling?" Captain Qonne demanded. He looked down at Gabe in a bird-like and predatory way. "This the larval thing endangering us?"

"This is Ambassador Gabriel Sandro Fuentes," said Kaen. Her face looked chiseled out of seriousness.

Gabe tried to stand with equal dignity. He was grateful that she came to his defense, though he also realized that she wasn't just standing up for him. She was standing up for his office, his title, his job—the one that she shared. *Not everyone respects ambassadors, apparently,* he thought.

"Greetings, Captains," Gabe said. He tried to say it as though speaking to peers—adult, alien, powerful peers.

The four captains watched Gabe without answering.

"Could kill it," said Qonne. "This thing could sleep

and trance, could still betray us in the dreams shared by all hatchling diplomats."

Mumwat spoke, his voice a deep rumble. "We have new understanding. Only accidentally did he interact with the Outlast."

Qonne was not mollified. His frown became a scowl. "Ignorance and blundering endangers us yet. Sedate it, if not kill it. Damage it into coma. Keep it from the dreams."

This is not going well, Gabe thought. He held the cane close, and wished the sword inside it were a useful defense against a holographic projection of the bird-shaped captain. *I thought that Kaen and I had finished this argument already.*

"The Terran ambassador now offers us guest gifts," Tlatoani pointed out. "He offers hospitality, and rights to the ice we have taken unasked. And I offered guest gifts in return when I welcomed him aboard the *Calendar*."

Qonne threw his words at everyone. "Endanger the remaining fleet to a hatchling, blundering and ignorant?"

Shame spread inside Gabe. Anger followed, and they fed on each other. He didn't try to ignore or suppress either feeling, and he probably couldn't have if he did try. Instead he held them close, held them still, and tried to stay calm.

Say something, he demanded of himself. *Talk your way out of this. Words are your weapons, the only ones you've got—except for the sword. Start talking.*

The Envoy spoke up before Gabe could.

"You cannot kill *me*." It kept its voice low, though furious shades of purple rioted across its skin. "I can scatter my own molecules at will. I can escape and subsequently regrow. I can steal one of your ships. I can build my own. I can launch myself through the vacuum of space without any ship at all, and still survive. You cannot kill me, or prevent me from returning to the planet that is my responsibility. If you harm this ambassador I will select another, and I will teach them that the Kaen are our enemies. I will teach them that the Kaen betray their own laws of hospitality and welcome, that the Kaen cannot now or ever be trusted. The new Terran ambassador will spread this knowledge throughout the Embassy, and throughout the galaxy. Kaen will become pariah, forever shunned, forever unwelcome in every sun, every system, every world. I will do this, and you will be powerless to prevent it, if you harm Ambassador Gabriel Fuentes."

Silence.

The Great Speaker smiled a tight-lipped smile.

Mumwat's suit creaked as he crossed metal arms. "I

move to honor the treaty negotiated by our own ambassador," he said.

"Agreement," said Seiba the floating guru-tree.

"Conditional agreement," Tlatoani said. "If his ignorance endangers us, then we should address that ignorance. During his time with us he should take housing in our own academy, and accept tutelage there."

I need to get home, Gabe thought, but did not say. The thought was a lump in his throat. He swallowed it. *But I also need to survive long enough to get home.*

Everyone in the room turned to look at Qonne's glowing projection.

"Three captains are agreed," he said. "This makes the decision. My voice is not required."

"I remain curious to know if you agree," Tlatoani said.

Qonne's projection disappeared.

"That answers that," Gabe said quietly.

Kaen gave a hum of agreement. "His people don't teach language at all until adulthood. It's what marks adulthood for them. So they never send children to the academy, and never become ambassadors. They don't respect ambassadors much."

Gabe knelt on the floor to be closer to his Envoy, whose skin still flowed in furious shades of purple. It clearly hadn't calmed down yet.

"Thanks," said Gabe.

"You are most welcome," it told him in his mother's voice.

The remaining three captains spoke among themselves.

"I go to stretch leaves in a window bubble and taste the outside light," said Seiba.

"We all hide inside an ice cave," Tlatoani pointed out. "You will have very little light to taste."

"A little always trickles in," Seiba said, and disappeared.

Speaker Tlatoani turned to Mumwat. "Will you stay aboard?" she asked. "You are welcome to swim in the irrigation lakes of Day."

"For now," he answered, and then addressed Gabe. "Welcome to the fleet. Pleased we are that we will not kill you, or damage your brain with deliberate intent."

"Thank you," Gabe said. "Likewise."

Mumwat crouched through the doorway and left.

Gabe stood to face the last remaining captain.

"Thank you for your hospitality, Great Speaker." He sharpened those words to very fine points.

Tlatoani smiled again. "Thank you for your own, and for henceforth avoiding the dangers of Outlast attention. I trust that you will make productive use of our academy, lacking one as your world does. And while in the academy you should hold conference with that other stray ambassador we found, the very pale one. When first I saw her I feared that volcanoes had covered up the old world's skies with ash, and that the only people to thrive below the ashes had become as pale as cave fish, desperate to absorb nutrients from whatever weak sunlight could still find them."

"The *other* ambassador?" Gabe asked. "What other ambassador?"

"That little mouth who names herself Nadia."

PART TWO
WITNESSES

7

Nadia Antonovna Kollontai went walking blindfolded through the streets of Night.

Rem the pilot and Dromidan the doctor went with her, though only Rem actually walked. Dr. Dromidan sat perched on Nadia's shoulder. The doctor tugged on her earlobe to warn her about bumping into things, and tried to convince her to take off the blindfold. Small, clawed hands reached out and tugged on the knot that kept the cloth in place.

Nadia stopped moving and shoved Dr. Dromidan off her shoulder. She heard wings flap around her head. The doctor landed on Nadia's other shoulder and punched her in the ear.

"Ow," Nadia said.

"Are you in pain?" Rem asked.

"Only from my doctor's care." Nadia rubbed her ear.

Dr. Dromidan untied the blindfold knot. Nadia didn't try to stop her this time. "Are there lots of people around?"

"A few dozen at least," said Rem.

"And we're near a translation node?" Nadia asked.

Of course we are, she thought an instant later, but she was nervous.

Rem added cheerful scorn to his voice. "No. We're nowhere near a public translator. You can't understand me at all. I'm free to point out just how silly you look with a piece of cloth wrapped around your face." Sarcasm usually translated poorly, but Rem understood it well. He could employ near-Muscovite levels of derisive mockery when he wanted to.

"Dr. Dromidan, would you go perch on *his* shoulder and punch the side of his head?"

"No," the doctor said, and continued to untie Nadia's blindfold.

She closed her eyes and tried to breathe in a calm and steady sort of way.

The blindfold came off.

"Look," the doctor said.

"Just a moment." Nadia stood and breathed.

"Look," the doctor said again.

Nadia opened her eyes.

She saw movement. She saw pale lights that she

knew were probably streetlamps. She saw the distant and reflected glow of Day above them. But nothing that she saw made any sense to her—especially not the other people out walking through the streets of Night. Translation tried to give everyone a familiar, human-like appearance that Nadia could understand, but Nadia no longer understood *any* visual information. Her eyes worked fine, but they refused to communicate with her brain. She scrunched them shut. Then she took the blindfold back from the doctor and tied it in place.

"No improvement," she reported.

She used to be an ambassador. She used to hold conversations across hundreds of thousands of light-years. She used to understand every gesture and expression that her colleagues made. But now visual translation gave her dizzying headaches.

Dr. Dromidan made a clicking sound of consternation. She patted Nadia's ear.

"I'm hungry," Nadia said. "Back to the big pyramid we go."

"I should return to *Barnacle*," Rem told her. "She's mostly recovered from the accident."

That's not quite the right word, Nadia thought. Experiment *would be closer than* accident.

"But she still gets fidgety if docked for too long," Rem

went on. "We need to fly a few laps around this little ice cave."

Nadia nodded and immediately wished that she hadn't. She still felt dizzy. She also felt like *Barnacle*: docked and stationary for far too long. "Tell the ship I said hello."

"I will."

Nadia heard the Khelone's heavy footfalls slowly recede into the crowd.

Dr. Dromidan tugged on Nadia's earlobe to let her know where the pyramid stood. Nadia walked in that direction. She trusted other people to keep out of her way, and they usually did.

Sound bounced and echoed inside the pyramid. Nadia could recognize most of the chambers and passageways by the way noises behaved inside each. She made sharp clicks with her tongue to feel out the shape of the space around her. Dr. Dromidan had taught her that trick. The doctor herself had large, unfolding ears and a more precise sense of sonar than any human could ever learn, but even Nadia's human ears found walls when she made clicking sounds.

"Good," the doctor said, noting her progress with echolocation. Then she tugged on Nadia's earlobe when she made a wrong turn and directed her into the shared kitchens.

Nadia was accustomed to the idea of shared kitchens. Her aunt and uncle's apartment kitchen in Moscow had been similarly communal, used equally by several different households—though some of those households had been more equal than others. Mrs. Lebedevo had carefully policed all of their communal supplies.

In her memory she heard heavy boots on a kitchen floor.

Nadia paused to shut down all thoughts of Mrs. Lebedevo, their shared kitchen, and the cupboard that Nadia had hidden inside.

"Hello?" she said to the kitchen. "Anyone here?"

She got no answer, and she felt out the familiar shape of the room from the echoes her voice made inside it.

"Good," she said to herself. She tried to avoid the kitchens during busy mealtimes, and she couldn't easily predict their timing. Different species lived according to very different rhythms. Some gobbled down constant calories like sugar-burning hummingbirds. Others ate rarely.

She avoided shelves of foams, sprays, and dehydrated tablets, each one engineered down to individual molecules and carefully labeled according to the species that would find them most nutritious. Nadia couldn't read the labels, and didn't want to anyway. The tasteless stuff reminded her of nonfood she had eaten at Zvezda.

Nadia preferred *food*, and she could smell some. An actual meal simmered on the stove, hot with energy siphoned from the apex of the pyramid. Nadia found a small bowl and followed the smell.

"Hot," Dr. Dromidan cautioned her.

"I know it's hot," Nadia said. "It's a stove. It's supposed to be hot."

"Glove," the doctor said.

Nadia lowered her blindfold. She looked at the stove and the counter beside it, but she couldn't actually *see* either one, or identify any specific object in front of her. She moved one hand over the counter surface, feeling for cloth, trying to find some sort of oven mitt.

Dromidan punched her in the ear.

"Ow!"

"Knife," the doctor said helpfully. "Sharp."

"They're supposed to be sharp," Nadia said. "But I wish people wouldn't leave them lying around. Okay, can you help me find a glove?"

Dromidan held her earlobe and used it to steer Nadia's hand across the counter until she touched an oven mitt. She put it on, lifted the lid from a simmering pot of tasty-smelling stuff, and then ladled the goop into her bowl without spilling.

The goop tasted splendid. Its rich intensity of flavors

almost made her cry. Nadia had no clear idea what was in it, exactly—some combination of corn, beans, squash, and probably chocolate. She was still amazed that corn could taste so good. In Russia corn meant failure, choking and terrible failure. Foolish politicians had tried to import corn as the new staple grain of the USSR. It did not work out well. Corn refused to grow in Russia. *But space is even colder,* she thought, *and the Kaen figured out how to grow it here.*

Dr. Dromidan flew from Nadia's shoulder to find something of her own to eat. Then she landed back again and made disgusting chewing noises right next to Nadia's ear.

Someone came in—a few someones. Nadia raised her blindfold to keep visual translations from failing, flailing, and giving her another headache.

"Hello," she said. "The stuff on the stove is delicious if you happen to be human. It might be poisonous if you're not."

"Hello, Nadia," said a very familiar voice.

She dropped her bowl and felt supper splash over her feet.

Uncle? No. He's dead. Uncle Konstantine and Aunt Marina are dead and a long way from here.

"Envoy?" she asked.

8

Gabe watched the former ambassador of Terra and all Terran life as she knelt down, found the Envoy with one reaching hand, and poked it where its nose would have been if the Envoy had a nose.

"It is you," she said.

"I'm so sorry I startled you," said the Envoy. It used a different voice, a deep and raspy voice, one that sounded nothing at all like Gabe's mom. "Now you're kneeling in a puddle of food."

"Don't care," she said. "And they keep cleaning towels around here somewhere. Over there, I think." The alien on her shoulder tugged her earlobe. Nadia adjusted her pointing arm. "Over there, I mean. I'm blind, by the way. Sort of. Mostly. It happened when we bounced off the lanes. Our experiment in sidestepping light speed didn't work very well. The Kaen fleet found us damaged and took us in."

The Envoy scootched closer. "You don't look any older than you did when you left."

"Rem said time might have gotten a little weird when we bounced," Nadia said, unconcerned. "I don't know what year this is, though. Even though we're on board a ship named *Calendar*."

The Envoy hesitated.

Nadia poked it again. "Well?"

"You left the moon forty years ago, Nadia."

She sat back on her heels. Then she laughed a sharp and pointy laugh. "I'm more than fifty years old," she said. "Strange. Do we have cities on the moon now? Has Zvezda grown up to become a thriving lunar metropolis?"

"No," the Envoy said. "Zvezda is as you left it, and empty."

"You're full of good news. Tell me that the USSR still exists, at least."

"It doesn't, I'm afraid," the Envoy told her.

"What?" Nadia demanded. "What happened? Nuclear war?"

"No, no, no," the Envoy said. "No. The planet is still very much inhabited and un-nuked. Russia is still there. But the USSR has collapsed."

Nadia took a deep breath. "It never held together very well anyway."

Gabe fidgeted, uncomfortable. *They're speaking Russian*, he realized. *I just hear the translation. Their accents sound Russian—maybe because I expect them to.* When the Envoy shifted the shape of its vocal chords it seemed to become someone else, someone Gabe didn't know at all. This was Nadia's Envoy. Gabe had no part in their shared conversation.

Nadia must have heard him fidget. She lifted her head. "Hello?"

Kaen spoke first. "Greetings, Ambassador Emeritus Nadia."

Nadia stood up. She might not be much older than Gabe or Kaen, but she did stand much taller. Spilled food stained the knees of her Kaen-style clothing. "Greetings, Ambassador Kaen," she said, mimicking the deep cadences of Protocol, the Embassy's own voice. "Who else is here? Somebody is. Someone else is breathing in a human sort of way."

Gabe waved, and immediately realized that she couldn't see his hand.

"Hi," he said. "I'm Gabe. I'm the one with your old job."

"Hello, Ambassador Gabe," Nadia said. "I'm relieved that you aren't Vanechka Vladimirovna. I suppose she must be too old by now. Would you mind finding a mop? Or just a cloth. They're somewhere over there."

* * * *

The three human ambassadors cleaned up the mess and then sat in conference over supper. The Envoy joined them, but Dr. Dromidan whispered something in Nadia's ear and then flew away.

The food itself was goopy and acceptable, though Gabe couldn't help imagining his father's disgruntlement. *Bland,* he would say. *Bland as shopping mall music. Bland as a blank Hallmark card. I traveled the world to learn how to cook. You'd think they would learn more exciting things about food while traveling the galaxy.*

Gabe held up his end of the imaginary conversation. *This is a spaceship,* he reminded his dad. *This goop is better than the freeze-dried stuff they eat on the International Space Station. It's much, much better than those leftover tubes on the moon base.*

The ambassadors told each other stories between mouthfuls. Gabe described his eventful and inauspicious beginning as the representative of their shared planet of origin. The story embarrassed him. His audience was intimidating. Kaen paid him chiseled, impassive attention. Nadia listened, blindfolded like some mythic spirit of justice and judgment, obviously amused. She had represented their world for years before leaving it. Gabe feared her opinion of his first few days on the job.

"At least you're still alive," she pointed out when he was done. "The planet is still there. The Outlast have yet to come conquering. Good enough. Nicely done. And I'm glad that you two didn't kill each other."

After supper she heated up some bitter and spicy drinking chocolate. The others all offered to help, but Nadia waved them away.

Gabe glanced at the wall of shelves and metal canisters. The labels rearranged themselves into words he could read: apple, mamey, sapote, potato, manioc, jicama, avocado, acacia, tejocote, plum, guava, cactus fruit. He wondered if farmers actually grew all of those plants in the fields of Day, or if laboratories grew the stuff instead. Each canister looked much too small to hold apples or jicama.

Nadia handed out drinking bowls of chocolate. The Envoy reshaped itself into a larger bowl, poured the molten stuff inside, and then closed up around the tasty pool and began to slowly digest. Gabe could still see the bubble of chocolate through clear purple skin.

"So now the fleet captains have sent you to the academy for babysitting," Nadia said to Gabe. "Could be worse."

"Could be much worse," he agreed. "They obviously don't trust any of us."

"They have little reason to trust you," Kaen pointed out.

"I guess," Gabe said. "But why don't they trust *you?* Their own ambassador?"

"Some are unhappy to be represented by a child," Kaen said carefully. "You saw that for yourself."

"Understatement," Nadia agreed.

"My predecessor was better at pretending that the captains could boss him around," Kaen went on. "He would listen, show them excessive respect, and then quietly do whatever needed doing—whether or not the captains would approve. But I don't know how to show respect that I don't actually have. If I think one of the captains doesn't understand the situation that they're trying to control, then my face says 'You're an idiot,' regardless of what I say out loud. That expression gets translated into every single language of the Kaen. The captains have little reason to be fond of me."

"Poor dears," Nadia said without sympathy. Then she laughed and sipped her chocolate.

She seems oddly content for someone who just found out that she's lost forty years, Gabe thought. *She isn't grieving for a lost home.* He wondered how he would feel in her place. He wondered how he was supposed to feel *now,* with house destroyed and family scattered. Right at that moment he felt nothing at all. Then he suddenly felt everything, and had to look away. He read canister labels until the feeling passed him by. Sapote, potato, manioc, jicama, avocado.

Gabe spoke up when he felt nothing again. "Nadia?"

She looked his way. No, she didn't *actually* look his way, but she did turn in his direction to show that she heard him. "Yes?"

"Your turn in the spotlight. Why did you leave?"

That question clearly surprised her. "Envoy hasn't told you? It should have."

Gabe glanced at the Envoy, who sat on the floor like a lump. Chocolate swished back and forth inside it with a soothing rhythm.

"I think it fell asleep," Gabe said. "And it hasn't had time to tell me much. We've been busy."

Nadia downed the thick, spicy sludge at the bottom of her bowl before answering. "Here's a quick summary, then. You've heard of the Machinae?"

Gabe nodded. Then he said, "Yes." Then he apologized for nodding silently instead of saying yes the first time. "I've heard of them, sure, but I don't know much."

"No one knows much," Nadia said. "They don't communicate with any other species or civilization. They don't even share our dimension, exactly. But Machinae space overlaps with our own. We call those overlapping places *the lanes,* and sometimes we can see Machinae moving through them. Now Outlast ships are traveling through Machinae lanes, *inside* the lanes. That's how they spread so fast. Galactic conquest shouldn't even be possible. The worlds are all too far apart. You can't send armies across thousands of light-years of dark, cold space. You can't send supplies after them and expect to reach them in time to be useful. You can't conquer the galaxy. It's like trying to invade Russia in winter. That didn't go well for Napoleon, or for Hitler. And galactic history hasn't smiled on large military campaigns either—not just because they were violent, wasteful, vicious, and wrong, but because they just don't work. The distance is too great, and too cold. No one can muster up the resources. No one can travel fast enough. But no one told that to the Outlast, and now they're doing it anyway. They're conquering worlds and systems at a steady, constant, *impossible* rate, and this is how. Ambassadors from the Seventh Fiefdom, the Volen Enclaves, and the People of the Domes all witnessed the Outlast emerge from the Machinae lanes."

"I haven't heard of any of them," Gabe admitted.

"Probably not," Nadia said. "They don't exist anymore."

"We saw it too," Kaen said quietly. "Their warships did come at us from the lanes."

"So I see two possibilities here," Nadia went on. "Either

the Outlast and the Machinae have some kind of alliance—which isn't very likely, since the Outlast are absolute crap at talking to *anyone*—or else the Machinae are ignoring this intrusion, just like they ignore everyone else in the galaxy. The Machinae might not have even *noticed* Outlast warships cruising by. Either way, someone needs to make contact. If the Machinae have an alliance with the Outlast, then we need to convince them to break it. If they haven't noticed the Outlast, then we need to convince them to notice. Someone needs to go talk to them."

"Which nobody has ever done before," said Gabe.

"No one," said Kaen. "Ever. And we're assuming the Machinae are even alive."

"All true," said Nadia, somehow unruffled. "And flying into the lanes did not go well the first time I tried it. But I come from a family of scientists. We act on what we know, and always know we might be wrong. I still need to try again, just as soon as *Barnacle* recovers from the last time. The ship is willing. The pilot is willing and even more eager. Test pilots are the same in any species, I guess. They love to strap themselves into something that might explode, just to do what no one's ever done before."

"A family of scientists?" Gabe asked. "So you do have family back home?"

"No," Nadia said. That word was a key, and she used it to lock all the doors and windows of herself.

Gabe quickly changed the subject back again. "So we need to accomplish various things that no one has ever done. Okay. Sure. How can I help?"

Nadia smiled wide. "You *are* an ambassador. You can play along. Others are likely to scorn a secret hope. Others would be quick to say 'No, that's just stupid.' But ambassadors can run with unfamiliar games. Ambassadors know how to play."

Gabe let out a breath he didn't know he was holding. For the very first time since his very first Embassy visit, Gabriel Sandro Fuentes didn't feel like an outsider. "So what's the next part of the game plan?"

"We may yet learn how to travel through the lanes," said Kaen. "If we can do that, we can outrun the Outlast. We can negate their advantage. Maybe we can find a way to slow that advantage or remove it entirely. Other civilizations have studied the lanes—Sapi's people most of all."

"Sapi lives on the other side of the galaxy," Gabe said. "The Outlast frontier hasn't moved nearly that far."

"They don't study Machinae to defend themselves from the Outlast," said Kaen. "They study the lanes and the Machinae because they're curious. But her people will also have to worry about the Outlast *eventually*."

"Okay," Gabe said. "So you're going to talk to Sapi, and I can help by asking around and finding other ambassadors who might know about the lanes."

"No," Kaen said. "You can help by coming with me and keeping quiet. Meet me at the lakeshore. Don't speak to anyone else before you find me there."

Gabe understood. He felt like an outsider again.

"The captains think I might do something stupid and dangerous," he said. "They told you to watch me in the Chancery."

"Yes," said Kaen.

Silence. Nadia broke it with a yawn. "I'm not sure what sort of sleep cycle you've got yourselves on, but it's bedtime for me."

"I'm a little bit exhausted," Gabe admitted.

"I'm not," said Kaen, "but this is a good time for an Embassy visit."

"Then off to the dorm rooms we go." Nadia stood. "I'll lead the way. I need the practice."

Gabe woke up the Envoy, who scootched groggily alongside. They all followed Nadia as she made clicking noises to navigate windowless hallways and passages.

She brought them to a small room with polished metal furniture and narrow sleeping nooks set into the walls—efficient storage shelves for sleeping people. The

Envoy ignored the nooks, rolled into a corner, and stayed there. Chocolate sloshed sleepily inside it. Kaen chose a nook near the ceiling and climbed in.

"This is your room too?" Gabe asked.

"It is now," she said. "Doesn't matter. They're mostly alike. And as current ambassadors—plus one former ambassador—we don't have to share rooms with any other academy students. Meet me at the Chancery lakeshore. Don't talk to anyone else."

"I heard you the first time." He tried to keep his voice neutral, but resentment still crept in.

Kaen didn't answer. She already slept.

"That was quick," Gabe said quietly.

Nadia sat in one of the metal chairs and took off her shoes. "You'll learn how to slip speedily into a sleep or a trance," she assured him. "Some ambassadors can even visit the Embassy while still awake and going about their business. They must seem distracted and daydreamy, though, splitting their focus between two places at once. I never learned that trick. But the trance is easier. Most of it is just breathing slowly. I'd teach you the basics now, but I'm too tired. The tree in the academy is much better at it. Learn from him. I go there sometimes to practice and help tutor the tiny ambassador hopefuls."

"Okay," Gabe said. "I'll ask Kaen tomorrow about

trances and trees." He fished around in his well-stocked emergency backpack for a toothbrush. "Is there a bathroom around here?"

"Down the hall on the left," she said. "Don't use water for washing up. There's a basin of disinfectant sand. Rub your hands with that. Be warned: Lots of species use that room, and none have very strong notions of privacy."

He expected Nadia to have claimed her own nook by the time he got back, but he found her still sitting in the chair.

"How's Earth?" she asked.

"Still there," he said. "Warmer since you left."

"What part are you from? United States? You sound like it, but translation does weird things to accents."

"United States," he confirmed. "Right smack in the middle of the continent."

"Well, I'm glad we haven't nuked each other. I don't suppose your country built any lunar cities while I was gone."

Gabe shook his head, and then remembered to say, "No," out loud.

"So NASA just walked around, took some souvenir rocks, snapped a few tourist pictures, and never went back?"

"Basically, yes," said Gabe. "I'm not happy about that either."

"At least you didn't nuke the moon," Nadia said.

"What?!"

Kaen rolled over, but she kept on snoring.

Gabe lowered his voice. "Why would we ever do that?"

"Just to prove that you could," Nadia said. "It was a pissing contest. The U.S. didn't know how to respond after we reached orbit first. You had to do *something*, and you decided to go walking on the moon. Good choice. I loved walking on the moon. But you almost detonated a nuclear warhead on the lunar surface instead, just to intimidate us with the sight."

"Are you sure?" Gabe asked. "How do you know?"

"It was an open secret," Nadia told him. "Or at least it was around my dinner table. Classified-but-not-really." She yawned again. "You should get to sleep. Kaen will be waiting. Say hello to Protocol for me when you get there. I miss him. Even though he's such a stuffy stickler for rules and procedures."

"I will," Gabe promised. He climbed into one of the lower nooks and tried to sleep, exhausted but also aware that he lay inside a pyramid, in Night and under Day, on a flying saucer, hiding in an asteroid, 266 million miles from Earth.

"Breathe slow," Nadia told him from across the room. She remained in her chair. In that moment she looked like she really might be half a century old.

9

"Greetings, Ambassador Gabriel Sandro Fuentes."

The voice came from every direction inside the welcoming chamber. Gabe watched his entangled sense of self take shape in the mirrored door.

"Greetings, Protocol."

"I trust that your earlier conflicts have been adequately resolved." It wasn't a question, but it was something very close. Protocol tried not to express curiosity. He was the place itself. He made communication possible, and considered it improper to pry or otherwise intrude into the actual *content* of galactic communication. But Protocol did sometimes strain against the strict parameters of his role.

"Adequately," Gabe agreed. "My very first treaty still holds, and no one is actively trying to kill me."

"Few forms of life can ever say the same," Protocol told him. "I hope that you savor your relative safety."

"I'll do my best," Gabe said. "And thank you for your help."

"You are most welcome, Ambassador. But please inform your Envoy that it should invest more time preparing its charges prior to their entanglement."

Gabe saw himself frown in the mirror, and tried to smooth it out into a neutral expression.

"I will," he lied politely.

"Proceed, Ambassador."

The door slid open. Gabe proceeded.

The Chancery stretched out in front of him. He set off for the lake, but he soon got distracted by a new game. It looked like some massive version of tag. Dozens of ambassadors chased dozens more across the open hills. Their clothes turned white whenever they got tagged.

One of the kids in white paused when he noticed Gabe watching. "Want to play?"

"What's the game?" Gabe asked.

"Outlast."

"How do you play?" Gabe asked warily.

"You run," the other ambassador told him. "If they catch you, you die. Then you have to play for the other side. The game ends when everyone loses. When only the Outlast are left. It always happens eventually."

Gabe watched some of the players get caught. They died with drama, loud and flailing. Then their clothes turned white, and the Outlast spread.

It looked like fun.

Omegan of the Outlast stood on a distant hilltop and watched, just as he always did.

"No thanks," Gabe said.

The other ambassador dashed off to rejoin the game.

Gabe found Kaen waiting on the lakeshore, impatient and annoyed.

"Sorry," he said. "Couldn't fall asleep."

"I asked you not to talk to anyone else here," she said.

Gabe wasn't sorry about that part. "Someone came and talked to me. I couldn't ignore them."

"Why not?" Kaen asked. "You can always pretend that you don't understand."

"We're standing in the middle of a massive and universal translation matrix," Gabe said. "How can I possibly pretend that I don't understand?"

Kaen shook her head. "No translation is completely universal. Just remember that I'm responsible for you."

"Sorry," Gabe said again. He tried to be sincere about it. He did try. "So where can we find Sapi?"

Kaen pointed at the lake. "Down there. At the very bottom."

Gabe considered the thick and viscous lake water. "Really? She strikes me as a more arboreal type."

"Really." Kaen walked down the sand bank and into the surf.

Gabe went with her. The water felt cool, but not cold. "How can we breathe down there?"

"Easily," said Kaen. "You really do need academy lessons. Your actual lungs are almost thirty thousand light-years away from here."

"I'm aware," Gabe said.

"So just dive down. Your projected self will acclimate to the new environment. This place would be less useful if we only ever spoke to ambassadors who happened to thrive in the same sorts of habitats. Here we can breathe underwater."

Gabe glanced at their soaring colleagues overhead. "Does that mean we can fly, too?"

"Of course," said Kaen. "Haven't you tried?"

"No. We've been busy."

"You should. But right now we need to swim."

She dove under the surface without bothering to take a breath first.

Gabe hesitated. The lake was deep, dark, and full of aliens.

He dove down.

* * * *

Breathing underwater is difficult when your body insists that it shouldn't be able to. Gabe hovered just under the surface, closed his eyes, and argued with his lungs.

We should panic, the lungs told him.

We'll be fine, he answered, and tried hard to believe it.

Start kicking back to the surface, they said.

You aren't even here, he reminded them. *You're very far away, along with the rest of me.*

We're sinking! his lungs shouted. *I really do think we should consider freaking out about this.*

Shhhhhhhhhh, he said. *Calm down.*

Both lungs continued to protest right up until the moment they relaxed into their usual rhythm.

Huh, they said. *That worked out fine.*

Gabe swam after Kaen.

She led them to a long stretch of sand at the very bottom.

Three other ambassadors stood there and yelled at each other. Sapi was one of them. She saw Kaen and Gabe, gave a joyful shout, and swam to catch them both in an awkward underwater group hug.

"I'm soooooooo glad to see you," she said in a muffled and watery voice. "I was worried. And I can't stand to be part of these talks anymore. Nope. Can't stand it. I need to tap out. Right now I don't care if they eat each other, and that makes me something less than neutral." She looked at Gabe and then smiled slowly. "Have *you* ever met those two down there?"

"No . . . ," Gabe said warily. "But I'm not really sure. They keep changing shape."

"They do that. One of them is Aza of the Ven. The other is Aza of the Gnole."

"They have the same name?" Gabe asked.

"Yes," Sapi said. "It's one of the many things they fight over. Do you have a vested interest in any possible outcome of their dispute?"

"Not as far as I know," Gabe said. "But what—"

"Do you even know what their dispute is?"

"Nope," Gabe said.

"Perfect!" Sapi looked gleeful. "Take my place. Mediate. Try to keep them calm. They shift when they get angry. I'm so very tired of hearing them bicker, and I need to go talk to Kaen anyway."

"But how can I mediate when I don't know what they're arguing about?"

Sapi patted the side of his head. "In this situation your ignorance is probably your strength. Have fun. Bye!"

Kaen and Sapi swam off, hand in hand.

Gabe floated down to stand on the lake floor.

"Hello," he said. "I am Ambassador Gabe of Terra."

Both Aza of the Ven and Aza of the Gnole tried to introduce themselves at once. Then the yelling started up again.

During the next few hours Gabe heard grievances, complaints, and accusations while Aza and Aza shifted shapes to become angular and toothy, or gelatinous and spiny, or massive and intimidating, or small and darting. Gabe's senses kept trying to translate their appearance into something he could recognize and understand, but they kept right on shifting and never looked human for long.

He did his best to keep them calm. He searched for the source of their shared animosity. He asked them to tell stories about an imaginary future in which they didn't hate each other. He told them to transform into shapes that would make the other laugh. Nothing worked.

Eventually Aza and Aza yelled themselves awake and both disappeared.

Gabe slumped down in the sand. *Well. That was an epic tantrum.* His whole body felt clenched, just exactly the way he felt after coaxing his twin toddler siblings through a solid hour of screaming and woe.

He wondered where Andrés and Noemi were, thirty

thousand light-years away from the Embassy. He wondered who was watching them, taking care of them right at that moment. Then he stopped wondering, because it made breathing underwater much more difficult.

Sapi and Kaen found him there.

"How'd it go?" Sapi asked, her voice perfectly cheerful.

"Badly," Gabe said. He didn't feel much like a qualified diplomat.

"Don't worry about it," Sapi told him. "Those two don't *want* to stop fighting. Not even a time-out down here in the cold and the dark could make them quit it. But there's still progress. Generations ago they were constantly trying to kill each other. Now they're constantly trying to humiliate each other. Maybe in another few generations they'll be the kind of buddies who constantly make fun of each other. Who knows?"

Gabe sat up and changed the subject. "I hope you two had a more useful chat than I did."

Kaen looked just like Gabe felt. *Probably not, then*, he thought. The other two sat beside him.

"Not very useful, no," Sapi admitted. "But it was still interesting. My people have studied the lanes and the Machinae for more than a thousand years. We're pretty sure the Machinae are artificial, or at least that they *used to be* machines, way down in the deep, dark days of their origins, before they went off on their own to become something else. Hence their name. And we've also bounced ships, sensors, and probes off the lanes to check out their strange, sneaky gravity. We think the lanes might be made out of gravitational bleed from another, adjacent universe, which is neat. That bleed might also be why our universe is speeding up as it expands, because otherwise it really should be slowing down by now. Also neat."

Kaen made an impatient noise.

Sapi spoke even faster. "But navigating *through* that overlapping space? Flying into the lanes? Nope. No idea how to do that. I'd say it isn't possible, except that Kaen here saw *someone else* accomplish it. So it must be possible. But we don't know how."

"Not even after a thousand years of study," said Kaen. Her voice sounded like a desert with no water anywhere, even while speaking at the bottom of a lake. She sounded empty of hope.

Sapi tried to throw a clump of sand at her, but the sand only scattered and floated away. "You make that seem like such a failure. It's not as though we weren't also doing other things at the same time. And curiosity narrowed down to one specific, practical goal misses out on all the good stuff."

"Right now I need to be practical minded," said Kaen.

"Of course you do," Sapi said. "I'm sorry. I can share all the details we've learned so far. Maybe you'll see something in it that we never did."

"Has anyone else studied the lanes?" Gabe asked. "We could compare notes."

Kaen shook her head. "We're not speaking of this openly. People have died for knowing what we know."

"People have also died for *not* knowing it," Gabe pointed out.

"We need to be cautious," Kaen insisted. "We need to keep this close. And I need to report back to the captains and reassure them that you're capable of keeping your head down, keeping quiet, and not putting the fleet in more danger than we already enjoy."

Gabe felt one bright flash of anger. "Don't threaten me. I've just heard two stubborn shape-shifters threaten each other, over and over again, for hours. Threats are just meaningless noise to me now."

"I didn't mean to threaten," Kaen said, her voice softer. "But the captains will ask. And I am a bad liar."

"I'm surprised," Gabe said. "You do have an excellent poker face. That's an expression for someone who hides secrets well."

"Good," said Kaen. "I've practiced that."

Gabe laughed and flopped onto his back in the sand. He watched lights and colors move across the upper surface of the lake.

"I should be going," Sapi said. "Now that Aza and Aza finally woke up I don't have anything else keeping me down here. And I don't like it down here very much. Hopefully I'll see you both next time I nap."

"We should be leaving too," said Kaen. "Lots to do, awake and asleep."

"Okay," Gabe said. He sat up.

The other two were already gone.

"I don't know how to wake on command yet," he said to the empty water where they used to be. He thought Kaen might physically wake him up after crawling out of her own nook, but that didn't seem to be happening. Instead he sat alone, surrounded by dark, cold water. Then he heard a low, gong-like noise.

Gabe recognized it as a summons. He swam for the surface and followed the sound.

10

The summons led Gabe to the surface of the lake. It led him across the beach and into the forest of silver leaves and oddly angular branches. His clothes dried quickly while he walked.

None of the other ambassadors seemed to notice the sound. He wondered if anyone else could hear it.

The summons ceased when he stepped into a small clearing and found his three neighbors there: Jir of the Builders and the Yards, Ca'tth of the Unbroken Line, and Ripe-fruit-dropped-in-sun-baked-mud-and-left-to-sit-content.

Ca'tth stood in the center with his shimmering eyes unfocused. He picked up a stick and used it to draw lines and circles in the dirt. The other two stood close by, tense and watching.

This looks like a private game, Gabe thought, unsure

whether or not to intrude. He drew closer. Jir noticed him.

"Get out," she said, her voice flat and wanting to flatten him. "You put us in danger. To play *catch*. You aren't welcome here. Not now." Her long hair snapped and cracked against the air.

"Noxious thing," Ripe agreed.

"No, no, no," Ca'tth told them, calm and quiet. All of his earlier, twitchy anxiety had fallen away from him. "Let the Gabe stay. The Gabe should know what's coming. Late, late, much too late to keep this hidden from his innocence."

He scratched out the drawings and then scribbled new ones in their place.

"Here and here," Ca'tth said.

Ripe shook his head several times.

"Are you sure?" Jir asked.

"Yes, yes, yes," Ca'tth insisted. "Go, go, go, go, go. My world has many hunting things. I know how to be hunted. I speak that language. Move your ships here, and also here."

Gabe felt a sinking feeling in his insides. *They aren't playing a game.*

"But they'll follow us," Jir said, her voice low.

Ca'tth tapped the scribbled drawing again. "They'll

focus on the planet and the larger ships. That's their pattern, one they always keep. You can slip away, both of you. Now, now, now, now, now."

Jir knelt down beside Ca'tth to be the same height. "But you're in one of the larger ships."

Ca'tth smiled. Gabe had never seen him smile before. "Go. This way and that way. Tell your ships which way to run."

Jir's hair lashed back and forth. "I'll have to wake up to do that. I can't daydream my way here like you can."

"Burning," Ripe said. "I smell burning in the air, in groundwater, in the ashes buried bitter in the dirt."

"You're getting older, Ripe," Ca'tth told him. "Your translations are slipping. Go find another world to put down roots." His ears fluttered. His eyes grew distant again. "The gaps are closing. Almost too late now. Wake up and be gone. Go very fast."

Ripe folded in on himself. He wrapped his arms around his legs and disappeared.

Jir looked at Gabe. He expected her to tell him to leave again. *Go. Get out. Not welcome.*

"Stay with him," she insisted.

Gabe nodded once.

Jir vanished.

Gabe and Ca'tth stood alone in the center of the clearing.

"What's happening?" Gabe whispered, even though he already knew. What he really meant to say was, "Here. I'm right here."

"Outlast," Ca'tth said simply.

This is what he was so terrified of, before, Gabe thought. *But he doesn't look scared now that it's happening. He's somewhere on the other side of scared.*

"I understand a hunt," Ca'tth told him. He kept his eyes closed now, focused on the things he saw while awake. "Hunters fixate, obsessed with just one thing at a time. I can work with that. Draw their focus. Demand attention. I can move as prey and make them follow me. No one else here knows what I'm doing. My shipmates think I'm using secret ambassador knowledge to plot our own escape. But I'm not. I'm plotting everyone else's escape."

Gabe tried to think of something comforting to do. Hold Ca'tth's hand, pat his shoulder, something, anything. He did none of those things. He had forgotten how.

"If the others reach my system, we'll welcome them," Gabe promised. "Help them hide."

"Thank you," Ca'tth said. "They *might* reach you, but it would take years. Outlast are more likely to find you first. I wish you a good hunt if they do. Be swift and clever."

"What can I do now?" Gabe whispered. "Is there anything I can do?" *Please give me something to do.*

"Stay right there," Ca'tth said. "Bear witness. Please don't go."

His stick still tapped in the dirt, but with less urgency.

"Now here," he said to himself, his thoughts very far away. "Now here." Then he dropped the stick. "Now."

Ca'tth's entangled self scattered and faded.

Gabe stood alone in the clearing, in the forest, in the Embassy, in the center of the galaxy.

"My fault," he said to himself. He had called them all together for a local game of catch. He invited predatory attention down on his closest neighbors. Now their homeworlds burned. Gabe would have thrown up if he had brought his stomach with him. "My fault."

"It is not," Omegan told him.

The Outlast ambassador stood at the edge of the trees. Gabe stared. He didn't know whether to attack him or run.

"We would have come for their worlds anyway, without that ball game," Omegan went on. "We had already fixed our attention there. You are not culpable in this."

Gabe did not find this comforting. Ca'tth was still dead.

"*You* are."

Omegan turned to go. "And for this reason you should not be speaking to me."

"How do you move through the lanes?" Gabe blurted out.

Sometimes the best way to know is just to ask, he thought.

Kaen is going to throw me out an airlock, he also thought.

Omegan turned slowly back around. "The lanes."

"The Machinae lanes," Gabe clarified. *If you really are sorry for this, then make some attempt to show it. Tell us what we need to know.*

"They recognize us," Omegan told him. "They let us pass."

I'm going to need more detail than that, Gabe thought.

"How? How did you make that happen? Did you speak to the Machinae?"

"No." Omegan struggled to find the words. "The lanes let us pass through. We did nothing to *make* that happen. Linked as we are, in the way that we are, in the way that we speak to each other, in the way that they recognized, the lanes let us pass."

I don't know what he's talking about, Gabe thought, frustrated and furious. *Is this a translation glitch? Maybe not. Maybe he just doesn't know how to say what he means.*

"How do the Outlast speak to each other?" Gabe asked.

"All at once," Omegan told him.

Gabe understood the danger then. Inside the privacy of his own head he said several scalding phrases he had learned from Lupe.

"Thanks," he said aloud, and then he woke up.

11

Omegan tried to hide what he knew. This was difficult. His species had always shared thought and experience with each other, each mind linked and entangled. They did not understand that other kinds of thought and experience had worth. They did not recognize anyone else's right to exist.

Omegan knew better. He was an ambassador. But ambassadors are juveniles, and easily ignored.

He hoped that everyone else would ignore him now.

The bond between Outlast grew stronger with age and maturity. Omegan was still young. He could still set his mind apart from their shared awareness. He tried to hide what he knew.

He failed.

Omegan woke. The clamor of all other Outlast voices echoed inside his head. They untangled in every direction.

The loudest voices set the shape of all the words to follow.

That one knows how we travel.

That one speaks with the Kaen.

Kaen survivors know how we travel, know and share the information.

The lanes.

The Machinae lanes.

Closed to all others.

Open to ourselves.

Chosen.

We forfeit all military advantage if we lose the lanes.

We forfeit all advantage if any others gain the lanes.

We forfeit the manifest certainty of our exclusive survival without the lanes.

We need the lanes.

We must keep the lanes.

We must find the Kaen survivors.

We must find those among them who share what they know.

Omegan failed to hold himself apart. But he noticed something that he had not known before.

Outlast had hidden themselves among the Kaen. Remnants of the last attack kept low and tried to discover their current location, the hiding place of all the Kaen survivors. These few Outlast had not learned it yet, but once they knew, all other Outlast would also know. The warships and raiders of the Outlast would come hunting for the Kaen.

Omegan became aware of these hidden Outlast, and in that moment they became aware of him and what he knew. They shifted their priorities and shaped their choices with new urgency.

The lanes.

Protect the lanes.

The Kaen must not learn how to travel the lanes.

Omegan could not hide what he knew.

I warned him, he thought, down in that part of himself where thoughts remained his own. *I warned the Terran not to talk to me.*

PART THREE
MESSENGERS

12

Gabe heard his mother's voice.

"Wake up."

He knew it wasn't her, but he took one long, drowsy moment to remember *why* it wasn't her.

"I'm awake," he told the Envoy.

"Excellent," it said. "We have breakfast to eat and business to attend to."

Gabe awkwardly crawled out of the sleeping nook set into the chamber wall.

He remembered the lake and the shifters, Sapi and Kaen, Ca'tth and Omegan. It still surprised him to remember his dreams. He never used to. Now he set these entangled memories gently aside.

Not yet, he thought. *Not yet. I can't sort through all of that yet.*

Someone had set out a change of clothes for him. He

put them on, relieved. His shorts and T-shirt had felt clammy ever since getting dunked in Minnehaha Falls. The Kaen tunic had far more dignity, and he was happy to borrow that dignity from them.

A platter of cakes that were *not* tamales sat on the floor beside a drinking bowl of water. *No one uses tables here,* Gabe grumbled to himself. *They have universal translators and artificial gravity, but no tables. Must be because the Kaen are all different species. Different heights. Waist high to me might be over someone else's head. If they have heads. Some of the people I saw in the city crowds yesterday didn't seem to have heads. Does the word* yesterday *still make sense when Night and Day are two constant, separate cities? Don't worry about it. Stop thinking in small circles and eat your breakfast.*

He ate all the cakes, because he was hungry, but they still tasted dry and bland to him.

"Where is everybody?" Gabe asked around an unsatisfying mouthful.

"Nadia is taking her customary walk around the city with Dromidan the antisocial doctor." When it spoke of Nadia, the Envoy slipped into a deeper, gruffer voice. "She has always enjoyed long walks. I hope she is well. I do hope so. Nadia is strong and stubborn enough to ignore her own injuries, which makes them unlikely to fully heal."

"Do you think her eyes will get better?" Gabe asked.

"No," the Envoy said. "And her eyes are not what I spoke of." It shook itself and reclaimed Gabe's mother's voice. "I'm unsure where Ambassador Kaen is, but she told me that she would return soon. She means to bring us to her academy, which is housed somewhere inside this large, pyramidal structure. Underneath the Library, I think. Ambassador Kaen intends to introduce us to her own envoy." It paused. Uncertain shades of purple flickered across its skin. "I have never met another envoy before. I'm not sure what this meeting will be like. Awkward, probably, given the fragile, tenuous levels of trust between ourselves and our hosts. I imagine Ambassador Kaen kept a very close watch on you in the Embassy."

Gabe nodded. "She did. But then, after she left . . ." His voice failed him. He cleared his throat, tried again, and broke off when Ambassador Kaen pushed aside the sliding door and reentered the room.

"What's wrong?" she asked when she saw Gabe's face.

So much, he thought. *And it's all mixing together. Ca'tth is dead. Dad's getting deported. My sister almost got kicked out of college before she could go. The twins are probably throwing mighty tantrums back and forth between them. Frankie's mom hates pets. She might have eaten mine by now.*

Mom doesn't know where I am, and not knowing probably stabs her in the stomach every single time she notices that I'm not there. These cakes are not tamales, not at all, and digesting them also feels like small stabs to the stomach. Many things are wrong.

He chose the largest and most immediate wrong to actually say out loud.

"Outlast just attacked the Centauri systems."

Kaen nodded. She held her head high and stuck out her chin, just like she always did whenever she decided to be brave about something. "That's close."

"Yeah," Gabe said.

"And heavily populated."

"Yeah," Gabe said. "Some ships evacuated during the attack. Others didn't. Ambassador Ca'tth of the Unbroken Line is dead. He sent out a local distress signal right after you woke up. I was the only one with him when he died."

And then I spoke with Omegan again, he thought. *I did exactly what I'm not supposed to do. But he told me something important. Something I don't understand yet. "The lanes recognize us. . . ."*

Kaen moved closer to him. She leaned in and pressed her forehead against his. Then she moved away again. The gesture seemed formal rather than affectionate, but it was still close.

"I'll let the captains know," said Kaen. "They should be preparing the fleet to run again, and soon, but we're still taking on supplies of ice. I'm not sure how quickly we can leave."

"You'll need to bring me home before you do leave," Gabe reminded her.

Kaen hesitated. "Even if the Outlast are coming? Even if they've already reached the Centauri systems?"

"Yes," Gabe said.

"Then I will," she said. "It was part of our treaty. Now come and meet the Envoy. I mean *my* envoy."

Elevator doors closed behind them. Kaen traced their route on the pyramid illustration etched into the wall.

"We'll have to pass through the academy," she said. "And we won't be able to talk along the way. The main floor lacks translation."

That seemed backward to Gabe. "Isn't translation a big part of our job?"

"Exactly," she said. "We don't want the little ambassadors-in-training to rely on it too much. Besides, everyone here is from the same fleet, whatever their ship and species of origin. We have a shared culture. They need to practice what it's like to talk to *alien* civilizations, so we make it harder to talk to each other. No translations, no explanations, no adult supervision. Not in the central chamber, at least. The little tutoring rooms off to the side have translation nodes. Former ambassadors serve there sometimes, and offer help when asked—but they have to be asked. Our envoy lives and works in one of those smaller rooms. That's where we're going."

"I have noticed that it doesn't remain by your side," Gabe's envoy said. "I find that surprising. Selecting an ambassador is the beginning of my task, not the end."

"No, it doesn't follow me around," said Kaen, also clearly surprised. "And it didn't choose me."

The Envoy turned shocked shades of purple. "But that selection is my primary responsibility."

"It considers *the academy* its primary responsibility," Kaen explained. "And the academy chose me. Our envoy met with every student and asked them to describe every other student, and whether or not they would make a good ambassador. It learned about us from what we said about each other. So *we* chose. It noticed that choice."

The elevator stopped. The door opened. Kaen probably said something like, "Follow me," but she said it in a language that Gabe couldn't understand.

The academy looked like a maze and an arena. Bright colors covered the floor and separated out different areas. Gabe saw holographic spaceflight simulators, hovering

four-dimensional puzzles, and kids of several different species gathered in a circle and singing—or at least he guessed
that they were singing. None of the noise translated.
None of the extraterrestrial Kaen looked human to him.

A long, narrow ball court took up the very center
of the room. Players passed the ball back and forth by
whacking it with sides, hips, and flanks rather than using
more nimble, articulate limbs to catch or throw. They
tried to knock the ball through mounted hoops, as in
basketball, but the hoops were twisted sideways, more
like tunnels than baskets.

Gabe recognized it. *This is the oldest sport we know
about. Mom just called it "the ball game." The Mesoamerican
ball game. People used to play it with thick rubber balls in
stone courtyards.*

"Hurry, Gabe," the Envoy said. "Our companion is
striding on ahead, and she hasn't noticed how far we lag
behind her."

"You don't sound like you want to hurry," Gabe pointed
out.

"I am feeling increasingly uncertain about meeting a
colleague," the Envoy admitted.

"I'm sorry you don't have all of this," Gabe said. "I'm
sorry humans burned down your academies. But I'm also
glad you stick around after you pick an ambassador."

"That is how I interpret my role," the Envoy said.

Kaen reached a door painted blue. She waited there for Gabe and his envoy before sliding it open. All three of them went in.

A dead alien lay sprawled across the center of the room.

13

The corpse was long, thin, and very pale. It had large, dark eyes and a small mouth, all open. Its two arms and hands looked similar to human limbs, though longer and with more joints. The rest looked far less human. Its torso ended in dozens of tentacles rather than legs.

"This was an Outlast," said Kaen, her words hard and sharp. "They boarded us in the last attack. We fought them off. Eventually."

Gabe stared. Then he almost laughed, and hiccupped instead.

Tentacles, he thought. *The Outlast have tentacles. Of course they do. Tentacled invaders on a flying saucer. All of our dreams and nightmares about space are true.*

"Why is there is a dead Outlast in your envoy's room?" Gabe asked.

"Because it's performing an autopsy," Kaen told him.

"Look. Here it comes. Look away instead if you're feeling squeamish."

An envoy oozed from a hole in the back of the Outlast skull. It was blue, bright blue, like turquoise or the Caribbean Sea, and its skin was covered in small, icky pieces of the corpse.

Blue Envoy oozed into a bowl of disinfectant sand and flopped around to scrub itself. Then it emerged and made a mouth. It didn't extend any sort of puppet-shaped limb, or take the time to mimic human vocal cords. Instead it just opened a mouth across its side. That made it look like a blue Pac-Man, or a beach ball slashed open. When it spoke it sounded like a toad.

"Welcome, Ambassador Gabriel Sandro Fuentes," it croaked. "I do apologize for the assassination attempts. It was I who sabotaged your device of entanglement from afar. The council of captains requested this of me, but my actions are my own and I must beg your pardon for them. I'm so very pleased that these efforts failed—due in no small part to brilliant engineering by your own envoy. I really don't know how it managed to maintain a stasis field around that tiny black hole for so long. Well done. Very well done."

"Thank you," said Purple Envoy, half-outraged and half-flattered.

"Consider yourself forgiven," Gabe said. "And you still have a smear of Outlast brains on your side. Over there." He pointed.

Blue Envoy scrubbed in the sand again. "Much obliged," it said. "Fascinating brain structure. The Outlast seem to have evolved a kind of cognitive entanglement, naturally occurring and shared throughout the species. Practically telepathic. Absolutely fascinating. But I would rather not carry accidental samples of brain tissue with me all over the place."

Purple Envoy scooted cautiously closer. "May I?"

"Yes, yes, of course!" Blue Envoy said, and oozed aside.

Purple Envoy peered into the skull cavity. It remained on the outside, looking in.

Something tickled in Gabe's own brain. *Linked as we are, in the way that we are . . .*

"What else did you learn about them?" Kaen asked, her voice still hard and sharp.

"A great deal," Blue Envoy said, "though I don't know how much will prove useful to us. The Outlast were aquatic in their recent ancestry. Now amphibious, they can move through many environments with ease."

It oozed around the edge of the room and adjusted a row of small and abstract figurines, each one carved of turquoise stone. Blue Envoy swallowed one of them, changed its shape by digesting part of it, and then spit the thing back out and carefully returned it to its place.

Maybe all envoys are sculptors, Gabe thought. *Mine made clay out of moon dust while stranded at Zvezda.*

"I can't tell if they are, or were, primarily a predator or prey species," Blue Envoy went on. "Likely both. And the workings and articulations of their limb joints are very interesting. I would like to describe those at length, but that would be indulgent and impose too much on your time. I didn't ask for your company in order to lecture you about Outlast wrist bones. I asked you here in order to introduce myself, and to apologize for my part in your attempted murder, which I've already done—and which I'll probably continue to do."

It's babbling, Gabe thought. *Maybe all envoys babble when they're nervous.*

"And you are still pardoned," he said aloud.

"Thank you," Blue Envoy said. "So very gracious. But I must also make some small amends for my actions by offering you . . . by making available to you . . ." It trailed off, embarrassed.

Purple Envoy broke the awkward silence. "You are repeating the Great Speaker's offer to make this academy and its tutors available to him. Because he has had no prior training, and very little instruction before the current crisis. None at all, really. But you fear that this invitation reflects poorly on me."

"Yes," Blue Envoy admitted. "And yes. But I don't want to cast any doubts or imply any criticisms of your work, I truly don't."

Purple Envoy bowed its head. "No offense taken. Truly. I *have* failed to maintain a proper academy on Earth, but that failure is not wholly my own. Human society has not tolerated any such institution so far. I am pleased to see that human ambassadors fare better here."

"Mostly," said Kaen. "But you've already seen that our society doesn't always respect us, either."

The two envoys huddled together and spoke of founding different academies. They paid less and less attention to anyone else.

Gabe and Kaen considered the dead Outlast and its broken skull. Kaen looked like she wanted to kill it again.

"Were you there?" Gabe asked. "When they attacked and boarded, were you there?" It felt dangerous to ask. Just asking might bring up wounds of blood and loss.

"No," said Kaen. "I was here. We sealed up the whole pyramid. Then we waited for a very long time without knowing much of anything about the fight, or about the rest of the fleet. We lost contact with each other. Ships scattered. And we couldn't find all of them when we gathered ourselves back together. We still don't know what happened to those missing ships. But we can guess."

"The Outlast don't ever lose contact with each other," Gabe mused. The tickle in his brain became an itch. "Not if they're all entangled. I wonder what that's like. Talking to everyone you know, all at once."

Linked as we are, in the way that we are, in the way that we speak to each other, in the way that they recognized, the lanes let us pass.

"What is it?" Kaen asked. "You're staring at an Outlast corpse with a huge, gleeful grin on your face, and I find that unsettling."

Gabe felt like shouting. He spoke softly as though sharing a secret instead.

"I know how they move through the lanes."

14

"You spoke to Omegan."

Kaen stood in a wide, solid stance, both arms to her sides, both eyes locked onto Gabe as though preparing to shoot powerful lasers at his face.

"Yes," Gabe admitted. "And he said—"

"You *spoke* to *Omegan*," Kaen repeated, as though no other information could possibly matter.

"Yes," Gabe said. "He spoke to me first."

"And you didn't leave? Run? Wake up immediately?"

"I didn't run," Gabe said. He didn't back down *now*, either. "And I don't know how to wake up immediately. Or how to fall asleep immediately. But I *would* like to learn, so if any academy tutors are available to show me, I'd be thrilled. I hear there's a tree who teaches the trance."

Kaen continued to glare at Gabe as though drilling ice out of his eyeballs. "So. You spoke to Omegan."

"Yes," Gabe said. "And he told me that the lanes recognize them. The lanes recognize the way Outlast communicate with each other. That's how they get through."

"You believe him." She said it like an accusation, like she also accused him of falling through infinite depths of stupidity.

Gabe nodded. "I believe him. He was horrified when Ca'tth died. He tried to comfort me afterward. He tried to convince me that it wasn't my fault."

Which didn't work, Gabe thought.

The two envoys abandoned their own conversation and moved to stand beside their respective ambassadors. Both kept silent.

Kaen shook her head. "The captains are going to kill us both. Or else force me to kill you while they watch."

Gabe wondered whether or not she was joking, or if this was something the Kaen actually did. He decided that he'd rather not know.

"Just run with this idea for a bit," Gabe said. "Please. Play along. You don't have to believe it, you just have to pretend. He said *recognize*. The lanes recognize them."

Kaen shifted her stance. It was slight. She just moved her weight between one foot and the other. But now the way she stood made her look less like a death-minded duelist and more like a ball player ready for a match.

Okay, let's do this, her stance said. *We aren't on the same team, but we're in the same game. I'll play along.*

"*If* that's true," she said, establishing rules and boundaries, "and *if* the word *recognize* translated well, then Outlast passage through the lanes isn't a trick of physics or engineering. They didn't build a new kind of ship, one that can travel through different kinds of space. They didn't *do* much of anything. The lanes decided to let them through because the Outlast are somehow familiar."

She paused. Gabe picked up the ball and ran farther. "The way they speak to each other is familiar."

Kaen caught his excitement. Her stance shifted again. Now maybe they could play on the same team.

"So the Machinae must communicate in similar ways. All together, all at once, all of them entangled."

Gabe waved his arms around like a happy Muppet. "*Yes.* And if that's true, if the Machinae *do* communicate, if the Machinae *can* communicate, then maybe we can figure out how to finally talk to them. Just like Nadia tried to do."

Kaen held up a cautioning hand. "That's still a huge leap to make. We can't even get into the lanes to have this impossible conversation. We can't pretend to be Outlast, or pretend to be Machinae. We won't be recognized. Not if we need to have brains shaped like that." She pointed at the broken Outlast cranium on the floor.

Purple Envoy tentatively raised its mouth. "And yet the both of you reshaped your neurology and perceptions in order to learn how to travel to the Embassy."

Blue Envoy spoke up with skepticism in its croaking voice. "Nadia Kollontai is similarly entangled, just as all ambassadors are. But when she tried to accomplish this the lanes refused her. She suffered injury rather than admission. Mere entanglement does not lead to recognition by the lanes."

"But she is not entangled like *this*." Purple Envoy peered back into the Outlast skull. "Not in the way you described. Most forms of life communicate in a linear, sequential sort of way. Their words move in straight lines, marching after each other in single file. A written book puts down lines of ink across a page like a train rolling down one single track. A line of spoken conversation lets all other branching threads, all the things that we might have talked about, disappear unspoken. But it seems that the Outlast can communicate in many directions at once—though only with each other, entangled as they are."

Blue Envoy started to bounce up and down. "We could

further adjust the speech centers of an ambassador's brain, one still young enough to have malleable neurology. If we used *every other* ambassador as fixed points of reference, and not merely the Embassy . . ."

". . . then we might create a massive, galaxy-wide synaptic map for language and meaning to play in," Purple Envoy added, finishing the thought. "The lanes might recognize such an expansively entangled ambassador. And the Machinae might speak with such an ambassador."

"That's a lot of may and might be," Kaen pointed out.

"Very true," Purple Envoy admitted. "All of this is wild conjecture and haphazard guesses, a number of *mights* fancifully piled on top of each other and teetering. It *might* be true and possible—but infinite numbers of things might be true."

"Agreed," said Blue Envoy. "We need evidence that this hypothesis is a coherent, workable theory before we risk tampering with anyone's brain."

"So how do we go looking for evidence?" Gabe asked. He felt his Muppet-flailing enthusiasm sink. "The only place we could go to find it is inside the lanes, and the whole problem is that we can't get there. I *could* ask Omegan for more details, but if I do that, Ambassador Kaen would have to kill me."

"That's right," said Kaen. "I would. So please don't."

Then she gave an unsettling smile of her own. "But there is someone else we could ask about this. We both happen to know an ancient artificial intelligence who holds billions of conversations at the same time. He hates to be pestered for information, but I think we should go and pester him."

Gabe was not at all sleepy. He felt the very opposite of sleepy. And he didn't want anyone to strangle him unconscious. So Gabe and Kaen went searching for the arboreal tutor who could teach him the trance.

The envoys stayed behind. They spoke very rapidly about new entanglements and bonded over other inscrutable, envoy-ish things.

"Why doesn't visual translation work on envoys?" Gabe asked Kaen as they set out across the main floor of the academy. "Neither one of them look human to me, even somewhere with translators turned on. They both still look like blobs."

Kaen just stared at him. Then she tapped her ear.

"Oh," said Gabe. "Right. Never mind."

They passed loud games and quiet games, simple games and complex games, contests, combats, and challenges, all unfolding around them in untranslated chaos.

Kaen led the way to another adjacent room. A huge

tree planted in a large, ceramic pot took up most of the space. The pot had wheels. Roots emerged from the edges and spread across the floor. Several small kids knelt around it, each one holding a root.

Nadia sat in a far corner. She held a tree root with one hand and fiddled with some sort of carved, tactile puzzle with the other.

"Ambassador conference first," said Kaen. "Then trance lesson."

Several students shushed her.

"And keep your voice down," Kaen whispered.

Once Gabe was inside the room the potted tree translated into something that looked more like a serene-faced dryad. It didn't seem to notice them. They tiptoed around tree roots and sat beside Nadia.

"Hello," whispered Kaen. "It's Kaen and Gabe."

"Greetings, Ambassadors," Nadia whispered. She set aside the root she held but kept fiddling with the puzzle. It looked like a ship, and then like a crouching animal, and after that like nothing Gabe recognized.

"We have lane-related news," Gabe said. "Maybe. Hopefully."

They took turns describing their teetering tower of mights, maybes, and guesswork. This time Gabe and Kaen played on the same team, tossing the ball back and forth between them as they raced ahead. Nadia listened, silent, and Gabe couldn't tell whether or not the older girl was willing to play. He tried to capture his earlier sense of excitement and expanded possibility. He tried not to feel foolish.

"I'll do it," Nadia said before they had even finished summing up the idea. She said it loudly. Meditating students shushed her. She showed no sign of noticing them at all.

"We haven't even talked about who would go through with this yet," Gabe said quietly.

"I'll do it," Nadia said again, softer this time. "If either one of you tries to go in my place I will break both of your legs in your sleep. This is mine to finish. Feel free to try it after I fail, but not until then." Her voice ended the argument. "So what happens next?"

Kaen took point. "Two things happen next: the envoys work together to design a new device of entanglement, and Gabe and I go to pester Protocol after Gabe learns the trance. Or we could make him run in circles until he exhausts himself and finally falls asleep, but this seems more efficient. And he should learn."

"He should learn," Nadia agreed. "Gabe, make yourself comfortable. Breathe slowly. Try not to think about anything."

"How?" Gabe asked, already frustrated by the thought of not thinking.

"You're about to learn how," Nadia told him. "Shut up and breathe. Then hold one of Kamalasil's roots. Tree species usually communicate through clicks and taps in their root structure. He'll guide you the rest of the way through the trance."

"Stay in the welcoming chamber when you get there," Kaen said. "I'll come find you." She closed her eyes, slowed her own breathing, and then went elsewhere. She didn't bother to hold one of the tree roots first.

Gabe sat up straight in what he hoped was a meditative way. He tried not to think about thinking. He tried not to notice other distractions like the sound of alien games outside or the sense that his other two colleagues judged him, impatient with his ignorance. He picked up a root and listened to the tutor's hypnotic voice. Then he forgot that he was listening. Gabe slipped into a trance and traveled.

"Greetings, Ambassador Fuentes," Protocol said. "I understand that you have questions for me."

Gabe opened his eyes. His entangled self stood in the welcoming chamber. Kaen was there already. She nodded, acknowledging his successful trance. It wasn't praise, but it was something close.

"Greetings, Protocol," he said. "Yes, we come with questions."

Protocol already sounded weary and put-upon. "I must reiterate that my purpose is to facilitate communication, not to participate in it directly."

"That's why we have questions for you in particular," said Kaen. "We need your help to facilitate a new and difficult kind of communication, one that has failed so far."

"Very well," Protocol sighed. "How may I be of service?"

Kaen and Gabe looked at each other, both unsure where to start.

"Are you Machinae?" Gabe asked.

Silence. They waited for an answer. Gabe almost repeated the question before Protocol finally spoke. "Yes. And also no."

Well, that was helpful, Gabe thought, but did not say. "Please clarify," he said instead. Protocol had a strong preference for respectful formality.

"Yes," Protocol said, "because the Machinae and I do share a common ancestry. We are both descended from the first forms of artificial life, built in the early, unremembered ages of the galaxy. And no, I am *not* Machinae. We are not the same. I remained here in the center. I have continued to serve my original function. But the Machinae moved on long ago. They made new functions and purposes for themselves. They have also drifted very far away from biological cognition, and ceased to send ambassadors here, to the Embassy, so I have no recent knowledge of them. Why do you ask?"

They told him why.

Protocol paused for another long moment, considering.

"You are correct," he said, eventually. "The Machinae are mutually entangled. This similar feature of the Outlast is likely what allows Outlast travel through the lanes. But I cannot speak to the merit of your plan. It *may* succeed. Entangled perceptions allow an ambassador to effectively experience two places at once; a more expansive entanglement may well provide the neurological architecture to think, and communicate, in many simultaneous directions. Your speech is usually so linear, but you may be capable of an expanding ripple of understanding rather than a single, plodding line of bread crumbs dropped and sometimes retrieved. But it is not my place to encourage direct action, and what you propose has never been attempted before. I advise caution, and I wish you luck."

"Thank you, Protocol," Gabe said. He felt like jumping up and down and running in wild circles. *This could work. It might not. But it could.*

"I also have a message," Protocol added. "Omegan of the Outlast has requested a meeting with you both."

Gabe and Kaen stared at each other, eyes wide.

"No," she said.

"It might be important," he said. "It has to be important."

"No," she said again.

"I don't think he means to hurt us," Gabe argued.

Kaen moved very close to him. "That doesn't matter. His intentions do not matter. Not at all. If you speak to him again, if you learn something from him, then he will also learn something about us—and anything he finds out, he'll share with other Outlast. He won't be able to help that. Nothing he has to say is worth the risk to hear."

Gabe desperately wanted to argue in favor of speech over silence. He silently nodded instead.

"Wake up," Kaen said. "We need to go back."

Gabe addressed the room. "Good-bye, Protocol. Please convey our regrets to Ambassador Omegan."

He closed his eyes, slowed his breathing, and left the Embassy.

Omegan stood alone by the lakeshore.

The others did not come. They would not come.

He kicked loose sand over the words he had written. He did not look down at them. He did not read or pay any particular attention to the words. He had drawn them in much the same way—idle, distracted, indifferent—such that any other member of Omegan's people, anyone aware of Omegan's awareness, might not notice what he wrote, what he tried to do, what he had failed to do because the other ambassadors did not come to read the words he had pretended not to write, the words he now erased:

Outlast on board your ship, hunting you.

15

Nadia went walking blindfolded through the city of Night.

Dr. Dromidan perched on her shoulder and tugged on her earlobe to steer them through twists and turns. Nadia suspected that they had made these turns already.

"Are we lost?" she asked, both amused and annoyed.

"No," Dromidan said, but then she tugged Nadia's earlobe in an uncertain way, without confidence or clear direction.

"Are you sure?" Nadia pressed.

The doctor tugged her earlobe the other way now.

Nadia sighed and walked that way. She wanted to ask for directions, but she didn't think the average passerby would be able to help. *Excuse me? Do you know where I can find the place where two envoys are building a very big machine? I'm sure it's around here somewhere. I know it's big. It wouldn't fit inside the pyramid. Or maybe they just wanted to hide it away so they wouldn't scare all those adorable academy kids by making my head explode in front of them.*

She should have accepted a formal escort surrounded by tall people with bright capes and brighter shields, marks of importance that she couldn't see. But Nadia wanted to walk alone, mostly alone, as alone as it was possible to be on a crowded city street with a grumbling doctor perched on her shoulder and pinching her earlobe with very small claws.

"Wait," Dromidan said.

"Wait for what?" Nadia asked. But the doctor flew off without answering, presumably to scout ahead. "Oh. Wait for you to come back. Fine."

She stood and she waited.

The place felt familiar. The pedestrian road under her feet felt familiar: firm but flexible, and probably made out of modified corn husks just like practically everything else here, from clothes to cups to plastic-like doors and windowpanes. The place also sounded familiar: the loud rumble of nearby speech, all translated, and the distant buzz of untranslated noise outside the range of the public node. It smelled familiar: the messy, greasy smell of a city in a warm season. In winter, in Moscow, the city smells vanished and each breath became sharp and clean.

But this city never knew winter, not when they kept their own small sun so close.

The place felt familiar, so she probably wasn't very far from the pyramid, but Nadia still couldn't tell where she stood, or where they were going. She waited, unhappy about that. She minded blindness less than standing still.

Rem and *Barnacle* also hated to stand still. So did the whole of the Kaen fleet, nomads with a shared culture shaped by more than a million years of galactic migration. No one here liked stillness. Nadia heard strain and frustration in the voices around her. She wondered if the people of Night really had somewhere to be, or if they just needed to go walking the way she often did, to move around while the ship and the fleet stood still.

"Nadia!" someone called. She wasn't sure of the voice, or even the direction it came from. Her name just emerged from the general hubbub. So she held up one hand and waved it, still standing in one place, still hoping to be found.

"Nadia," the voice said again, closer now. "It's Gabe. What happened? Did you get lost?"

He sounded so young. Nadia felt fifty years older. Which she was. Sort of.

"No," she said. "But my doctor did."

Dromidan made an indignant noise as she flew back to Nadia's shoulder.

"There she is," Nadia said. "Lead on, Ambassador Gabe."

He led them to an old textile factory. He walked with a cane. Nadia could hear the thunk of cane tip against corn-grown pavement.

She clicked her tongue once inside the factory. The walls took a long time to send answering echoes. "This place is big," she said.

"Very big," Gabe said. "Machines here used to make clothes and blankets out of spun corn silk, but the envoys took those apart, added bits and pieces of other things, and used them to build a massive device of entanglement."

"What does it look like?" Nadia asked.

"Like mad science," he told her. "Both envoys are climbing all over it like squirrels made of goo. Bright red sparks are shooting out like fireworks."

Nadia grinned. "This description fills me with confidence."

"Sorry," Gabe said. "It looks very safe. Polished, clean, and professional. Like a doctor's office. Yes. Of course it does."

"You've obviously never been to Moscow," she said, "because I've never seen a clean or polished doctor's office."

"Nope," Gabe said. "I'd never left the U.S. before I left the planet."

"You probably couldn't get a visa, anyway," Nadia said.

"It was easier to get to the moon than it would have been for me to cross borders."

"Likewise," Gabe said.

He sounded sad. Nadia respected his privacy and did not ask why. Instead she went toward the sounds of small explosions and metallic clanking. She trusted Dromidan to warn her before she stumbled into things. Then she heard an envoy move across the floor.

"Hello, Nadia," said Uncle's voice.

"Hello, Envoy." She knelt beside it. "How's progress?"

"The device is complete," it told her. "We have subjected its systems and subsystems to every test we could come up with. I think it will work. I do. But I might be wrong."

"That's always true," she said. "We might be wrong about everything we think we know. But we still have to work with it."

"You sound more like Konstantine than I do," the Envoy said.

She found it by touch and poked the place where its nose would be. "Let's get started."

"Now?" the Envoy asked. "Are you certain? And must *you* volunteer? There are other former ambassadors here in the fleet."

"Too old," she said.

"We could select a new ambassador from the academy, and advance them through multiple stages of entanglement."

"Too young," she argued.

"*Must* it be you?" it asked.

Nadia stood up and stopped arguing. "Poyekhali," she said instead.

"Then here we go," the Envoy said. "Please follow me. Reach out your hand and I will make a hand to hold it."

Ambassador Gabe, Ambassador Kaen, Captain Mumwat, and the Great Speaker Tlatoani all offered formal thanks and wishes for good luck. Nadia accepted them with practiced, formal grace while only half listening. She devoted the other half of her listening to the whirring, clanking hum of the entanglement device.

I wonder what I'll be when this is done, she thought.

The Envoy led her inside the device. It said more kind things that Nadia genuinely tried to listen to and still forgot immediately. Then it said, "Repeat after me: I will speak for this galaxy."

She smiled. "I, Nadia Antonovna Kollontai, will speak for this galaxy."

The Envoy closed her up inside the device of entanglement.

Something bothered her about that small space,

something that had nothing to do with the machine itself, but she didn't understand or remember until after the hatch closed and she heard her own breathing bounce between very close walls.

Aunt Marina and Uncle Konstantine had shoved her into the old kitchen cupboard, and that confined space had felt very much like this.

Nadia locked all the doors to that memory. Then she heard screams and shouts from outside the entanglement device.

All the locked doors of her memory broke.

"Hide and be silent," Aunt Marina pleaded.

Nadia refused to be silent. "What's going on?"

"Politics," Uncle Konstantine told her. "Ugly and ordinary things. Someone wants my job. The program fired Vasily Mishin and replaced him with Glushko—which is good, because Mishin's an idiot who keeps forcing us to use the wrong fuel. Glushko is a better man and a better engineer. But now there's a mess of rumors and maneuvering. Now someone wants my job."

"So why do your office politics mean 'It's time to stuff Nadia in a cupboard'?" she demanded.

"Because those rumors accuse us of conspiracy. And Judaism."

"We are Jewish," Nadia pointed out.

"And that truth might make the conspiracy charge stick," Uncle complained. "The NKVD are coming to ask questions, so please hide next to the pots and pans and make no noise whatsoever."

Narodny Komissariat Vnutrennikh Del. Secret police. The kind who came to make you disappear.

Uncle Konstantine shut the cupboard door.

Nadia hid. She remained silent. She heard the sound of heavy boots. Then she heard screaming and shouts from outside.

The massive entanglement device roared around her.

Her fists thumped against the flat metal walls.

"What's happening?" she yelled.

Then she saw light, bright through her eyelids and the blindfold she still wore.

Mrs. Lebedevo found her in the kitchen cupboard. Mrs. Lebedevo had been, in Nadia's usual experience, a horrible person. She was someone who complained loudly and often about Jews and the mysterious Jewish doctors she believed would someday poison her. She was someone who glared at the kinks in Nadia's hair. And whenever Mrs. Lebedevo complained about doctors and poisons,

Nadia would say nothing, absolutely nothing, all of the nothing that she knew how to say. Horrible old Mrs. Lebedevo found her alone in the cupboard, and made her tea that wasn't poisoned, and asked her if she had anywhere to go. Aunt Marina and Uncle Konstantine were gone already.

Nadia thanked her politely, and said that she did have somewhere to go. This was true. It was somewhere very far away. She had been planning that trip for over a year, and she had intended to tell her aunt and uncle about it before leaving. She had wanted to introduce them both to the Envoy, her mentor, her closest friend, the lump of purple goo who hid inside the floor of their apartment. She had hoped to ask for their help stowing aboard the last of the N-1 rockets. She had hoped to say good-bye, but she never got the chance.

The men took other things along with Aunt Marina and Uncle Konstantine. Nadia found the dusty outlines of books no longer on the shelves. She found footprints of dirty, melted snow on the carpet. The men had not wiped their boots.

The Envoy oozed its way up through a crack between floorboards, and the two of them sat in silence for a long time before they set their plans in motion. Then the Envoy spent hours on the phone. It mimicked the voices of many important people to learn what they needed to know.

Nadia gathered together their stolen supplies, all smuggled away from Uncle's lab: cans and tubes of food, tanks of oxygen, and Cosmonaut Valentina Tereshkova's spare suit. Stealing the suit had been especially tricky.

"They have tried to cancel the next launch," the Envoy told her. It still held the phone, and it still used Uncle Konstantine's voice to speak. Nadia tried to ignore how that made her feel. She also tried to embrace how it made her feel. "They don't want to bother racing to the moon now that the Americans have been there already."

"Americans just walked around and took pictures," she said. "But we have a moon base. We're going to build a whole city there."

"Not now," the Envoy said. "They've given up on the moon. I pretended to be the new chief Glushko. He has been here for drinks often enough, and his loud bluster is easy to mimic. I insisted that the scheduled launch move forward, but the deception won't last. Even if it works, this will be the final N-1 rocket before all lunar operations shut down. This is our last chance to reach the moon. We should hurry. We need to leave now for the launch site."

Nadia agreed, but she did not move. "What else?" she asked. "What happened to them?"

"Officially, nothing has happened," the Envoy said. "Absolutely nothing. Konstantine and Marina have simply disappeared."

"Can you make more phone calls and get them unofficially released, then?"

The Envoy took its time inhaling a large air bubble to speak with. "No," it said, gently. "I cannot."

Nadia bit the inside of her mouth, very hard. Then she kicked the bag. She tried to say "Get in," but the words refused to come. The Envoy understood anyway, and climbed inside.

She turned her back on her apartment home. She dragged the duffel behind her. In a full G it was too heavy to lift. This must have been uncomfortable for the Envoy inside, but it did not complain.

They climbed aboard a train. Then, early the next morning, they climbed into a cramped capsule inside a massive rocket and flew to the moon.

Now Nadia crouched inside the entanglement device and yelled.

No one answered.

16

The floor trembled as though shaken by an earthquake. Artificial gravity flailed, unable to decide how heavy anything should be. Gabe felt lighter, and then very much heavier. He held on to his great-grandfather's cane to keep it from floating away. Then he held on to keep himself from falling over.

Speaker Tlatoani pressed her hand against a circular screen set into the wall. Captain Mumwat joined her there. A series of glyphs appeared on the screen. They flickered into words Gabe could read and then back again before he actually read them. Mumwat's visual translation also fluctuated. He looked human in one moment and more like a suit of armor with a fishbowl belly in the next.

The massive device continued to whirr and hum with Nadia inside. Gabe had no way to know if she was okay in there, and no one to ask. Both envoys climbed all over it, furiously working.

Kaen and Gabe shared a look, but neither tried to speak.

Gabe waited to understand.

He did not enjoy this kind of waiting.

Maybe the Outlast found us. Maybe the asteroid is collapsing. Maybe the ice cave is actually a giant space worm.

A man and a woman, both human adults, came bursting into the room. They exchanged hasty words with Tlatoani and then stood by the only door. Each removed a metal rod from an arm brace. The rods telescoped into short spears, and the braces expanded to become shields. Bright colors flickered across each shield, distracting and hypnotic.

Both gravity and translation stabilized. The captains left the wall panel to join the ambassadors.

"Sunset," said Tlatoani. "Our jaguars and ocelots paint with snake blood."

"Translation help?" Gabe whispered to Kaen. "Are we under attack?"

"We're under attack," she told him.

"Outlast?"

"I assume," she said, her voice flat and cold. "This is what happened the last time they found the fleet. We locked ourselves down and we waited."

"To our understanding the Outlast have *not* found the fleet," said Captain Mumwat in his rumbling voice. "No other ships report attack. This one alone, and only from inside. *Calendar* suffers from parasite infections, from stowaways and saboteurs."

Gabe heard screams and shouts outside the single door.

The two guards held up their weapons and stood ready.

"Spears and shields?" Gabe wondered aloud. "No guns? No blasters?" He didn't like guns very much, but he thought they would be useful now.

"Projectile weapons?" Tlatoani asked, unimpressed. "Did that translate correctly? Astonishingly ignorant to wish for projectile weapons inside a spacefaring ship. You make my face narrow. Devote yourself to a better understanding of physics if you survive long enough to learn."

Gabe drew his own elegant weapon. "I'll be sure to do that," he said, his voice wry and dry.

Purple Envoy dropped to the ground, flattened into a puddle, and then picked itself up. "We must keep the device undamaged," it said. "The process can't be interrupted now that it has begun. To do so would cause Nadia terrible harm."

Red sparks burst from the device. The Envoy went quickly back to work.

The door distended with a horrible shrieking sound.

Translation died. Both Kaen and the Speaker said things that Gabe could not understand. Mumwat swam in circles, agitated in the bowl-belly of his armor.

The door fell forward into the room, followed by Outlast.

They had long necks and long fingers, dark eyes and open mouths on pale, bald heads, and they glided smoothly into the room on dozens of tentacles. They leaned forward like bicyclists moving at very high speed.

Translation flickered on and off again. For a single moment Gabe saw the Outlast as human. He saw them as men in combat gear, white men with white letters that spelled ICE across thick, black vests. He saw them as the things he feared most. Then heavy boots became writhing tentacles again.

One of the invaders flexed long fingers as though cracking knuckles. Tiny arcs of lightning leaped between its fingertips.

The fight began.

Gabe saw spearheads connect and give off sudden bursts of energy. He saw Mumwat hoist up the Outlast, one in each robotic hand. They sent lightning from their fingertips into his arms, but that didn't seem to bother him down in his belly-bowl. He tossed them through the open doorway, picked up the fallen door, and held it back in place.

The male guard was down, but still breathing. He had raw burn marks around his neck. Kaen and Gabe helped him to his feet. He fell down again. Then he handed both spear and shield to Kaen before stumbling far from the door.

He can't fight anymore, Gabe thought. *He can't help, and he knows it. So now he just needs to get out of the way.*

Kaen held the shield up in front of them both. She said something. Gabe felt as though he understood the words, even though he didn't. The two ambassadors faced the doorway and waited for one long moment.

That moment stretched until it broke.

Pale hands and tentacles wrapped around the edges of the door, sparking like electric eels. The remaining guard attacked the tentacles with her spear. Kaen did the same. Gabe yelled something he hoped sounded fierce and stabbed at the reaching limbs with his sword.

Tentacles translated into boots kicking down the door, and then became tentacles again. They wrapped around Mumwat's wrist and broke his grip. The slab of metal fell back. It fell against Mumwat and shattered his fish-bowl. The empty suit collapsed. Mumwat lay flopping in a puddle on the floor.

Gabe tried to reach the aquatic captain, though he

didn't know what to do or how he could possibly help when he got to him.

His feet left the floor and kicked empty air.

Tentacles pinned his arms together. They lifted him higher and squeezed. Gabe dropped the sword. He couldn't breathe.

Kaen climbed the wreckage of the broken door. She had lost her spear, and her shield, but she used the cane sword to stab the Outlast through the eye.

It fell. Gabe fell with it.

Get up, he thought as he struggled to climb out from under dead tentacles. *There'll be more of them. They fight in numbers. They fight to overwhelm. Get up.* But he didn't hear any scuffles or slithering. He didn't hear screams outside the room, or shouts of alarm inside. He didn't hear anything but his own hasty scramble to get away from the dead things sprawled on the floor like the ropes of a mop head.

Kaen helped him up. The two of them stood beside Mumwat, who did not move.

Gabe suddenly knew what to do about that.

"Envoy!" he shouted.

Purple Envoy jumped from the device, flattened itself into a gliding shape, and flew across the room.

Gabe pointed at Mumwat. "Fishbowl," he said. "Like the bubble helmet you made for me, but the other way around."

Purple Envoy didn't waste time answering. It absorbed the spilled puddle. Once it held a big enough bubble of liquid it rolled over Mumwat and surrounded him, too.

The captain floated without moving. He rolled upside down. Then he twitched, fluttered fins, and began to swim in very small circles. He didn't have very much room to move in there.

I BELIEVE YOUR IDEA WORKED, the Envoy wrote across its own skin in glowing purple letters.

Gabe stopped holding his breath. He shared a look with Kaen, who still held the sword. Then he glanced at the entanglement device, which clanked, whirred, and sent red sparks in all directions. Blue Envoy continued to fiddle with it.

"How's Nadia?" Gabe asked.

UNKNOWN, Purple Envoy wrote. WE CAN'T KNOW UNTIL THE PROCESS IS COMPLETE, AND THAT WILL STILL TAKE SOME TIME. BUT AT LEAST IT CON- TINUES UNINTERRUPTED. THIS IS A TREMENDOUS RELIEF TO ME.

The uninjured guard stood watch in the broken door- way. Kaen joined her there. People of all different species moved in the street outside. None of them were Outlast. All of them stared upward.

Gabe went to see why.

Smoke billowed from the bowl above the pyramid, high above Night and high above Day. It formed dark, swirling clouds in the space between the two cities.

Oh no, he thought. *They broke the sun.*

Huge cracks and fissures marred the massive bowl at the apex of the pyramid. Glowing sun stuff spilled out like lava. Gabe thought it would pour down the sides, transforming the pyramid into a volcano and roasting everyone within. But the glowing liquid did not pour into Night, or drip from the bowl into Day. Instead it swirled away sideways, caught between two gravities. The clouds burned. The sky burned between Night and Day.

Gabe watched it happen until he couldn't watch anymore. Then he went back inside and picked his way between the fallen Outlast.

One of them moved.

Gabe shouted. He didn't know what he shouted, exactly, and without translation it didn't really matter.

Tentacles reached for him, and for Kaen, who answered with Toledo steel. Then the guard whacked the Outlast with the side of the spearhead she carried. Bright energy burst between weapon and skin. The Outlast slumped. The guard methodically secured its many limbs with some kind of foam.

Still alive, Gabe realized. *We have a prisoner.*

PART FOUR
NOMADS

PART FOUR

Fictions

17

Three ambassadors stood in the Chamber of the Homeworld, inside the House of Painted Books, inside the Temple of the Sun, underneath a cracked and hastily repaired bowl of burning solar stuff.

Gabe looked at the floor, a tiled mosaic of their shared planet of origin. All three of them stood on the swirling blue tiles of the Pacific Ocean. He looked at the walls, where an unfurled, accordion-bound book told of how humans first left Mexico to go migrating through the galaxy as members of the Kaen.

The four captains stood on the other side of the room and argued with Kaen's Blue Envoy.

They argued about the ambassadors. They also ignored the ambassadors. Gabe, Kaen, and Nadia stood by and listened. Gabe and Kaen listened, anyway; Nadia seemed distant and distracted behind the cloth of her blindfold—even more so than usual.

Maybe her new entanglement worked, Gabe thought. *Maybe. It didn't make her head explode, anyway. But she seems a bit spacey. And we won't really know if this worked until she tries to meet with the Machinae. And she won't get to do that unless the captains let her go.*

He considered the captains.

Mumwat still swam inside the bubble created by Gabe's Purple Envoy. He looked uncomfortable. The Envoy probably wasn't comfortable with this temporary arrangement, either.

Speaker Tlatoani looked stern and coldly angry. This was her ship, her home, her broken sun.

Seiba projected her translated image. She looked serene, and spoke softly without gestures. Gabe could barely hear her.

Qonne did most of the talking, anyway. He had come in person this time, and his voice sounded high and sharp like a bird of prey.

"This procedure, it was done without our sanction."

"It did not require your sanction," the Blue Envoy said in its toadlike voice. "This was the business of ambassadors, conducted by ambassadors. But Captain Mumwat and Speaker Tlatoani were both present to bear witness."

"Done without the sanction of the full four captains."

"You may continue to repeat that objection if you like, Captain Qonne," the Blue Envoy croaked politely. "It will remain both factually accurate and utterly irrelevant."

"The attack, the ambush by hidden Outlast—your actions brought it down upon us," Qonne said, seething.

"The business of ambassadors brought it down. *Our* business is to defend from such attacks."

"I agree," said Blue Envoy. "And I understand that you are frustrated by your failure to defend us. Please refrain from inflicting those frustrations upon others, or further exercising your authority over ambassadorial matters—especially given the fact that the ambassador emeritus who passed through an additional entanglement procedure is an honored guest of the Kaen. She is not of the Kaen. She does not represent the Kaen. She is not subject to the Kaen."

Gabe winced. So did Kaen.

"That's not going to help," she whispered. "He won't respond well to rebukes."

"I don't think he likes to be reminded about things beyond his control, either," Gabe whispered back. "He's already upset about just how much he can't control."

The bird captain raged in loud response. Gabe and Kaen shared a look. *Knew it.*

Nadia made a pained noise.

"You okay?" Gabe whispered.

"That voice," she said. "Words like frustrated flies whacking themselves against windows. Buzzing. Loud. Unable to understand the fact that glass exists."

Uh-oh, Gabe thought. *Giving her an extra-special dose of entangling was supposed to make her better at communication. She seems worse instead.*

"Right," he said aloud. "Yes. Annoying voices are arguing. True."

Qonne continued to bluster. Gabe understood less and less of it. "Kaen, are you catching any of this?"

"Some," she said, her voice a blunt weapon. "He thinks it's a terrible idea to send a 'hatchling,' a 'larval individual,' on a mission of first contact to the Machinae, especially one whose neurons we've just scrambled. He wants to send an adult instead."

Blue Envoy continued to argue in an impatient, croaking voice. "We cannot send an adult of any species into the lanes. Only someone young, someone whose neurological connections remain flexible and adaptable, can even undergo this procedure. Only a former ambassador can do so. It builds upon previous entanglements."

Captain Qonne remained adamant. "You cannot endanger another hatchling."

"Endanger," Gabe mused, his voice low. "Interesting choice of words."

"Condescending and insulting choice of words," said Kaen. "I'll walk out of this meeting if he says the word *hatchling* one more time."

"What do you think they're really arguing about over there?" Gabe asked.

"What is Qonne afraid of, you mean?" Kaen asked.

"I guess so," Gabe said. "Loss of control seems to be most of it."

"And trusting a child," said Kaen.

"*Endangering* a child," Gabe added. "He's not just trying to shut us up and make us go away. He might be trying to protect us—which I find hilarious, since he wanted to kill me earlier."

"How kind of him to protect us," said Kaen. She had her own history of disgruntlement with these captains—Qonne in particular. But then she looked thoughtful. "We might be able to use that. Qonne *needs* to be protective. He needs to exercise more control. We could offer him the chance."

"Sounds perfect," Gabe said. "How?"

"I don't know," she admitted. "Ideas?"

"No," Gabe said. "Wait, yes. Maybe. The prisoner?"

Kaen understood. "Perfect."

She cleared her throat and straightened her spine. Most species notice a more alert posture; whoever held such a posture might either run or pounce.

"Captain Qonne," she said, loudly. "I would speak."

The room fell silent. Qonne paused before answering. He clearly did not enjoy speaking with a child. Children of his species did not know how. "Speak then," he said. "Ambassador," he added once he remembered that he should.

Kaen spoke, slow and clear. "Nadia Kollontai *may* now be able to travel the lanes. The Outlast can *certainly* travel the lanes, and we hold a living Outlast prisoner. We could send this prisoner with her. Captain Qonne, would you be willing to contribute another passenger, someone from your own ship, someone capable of safely guarding the imprisoned Outlast?"

She phrased the idea tentatively, as a suggestion and a question. *That's not how she usually talks,* Gabe noticed. *She likes clear statements of fact. Instead she invited the captain to take up her idea and call it his.* He could tell that it bothered her to do this, but she did it anyway.

Qonne looked thoughtful. "Four captains will now consider this." That wasn't a yes, but it wasn't a no, either.

The four captains considered and deliberated at the far end of the chamber. The Blue Envoy left them there and scooted over to join the ambassadors.

"Well done," it said. "Very well done. You are all politicians."

Nadia flinched as though slapped. She turned to pay closer attention. "Where I come from, that word is an insult. It means someone powerful, privileged, fickle, and probably stupid. Someone who might have you killed for no reason."

Kaen's envoy turned embarrassed shades of blue. "Then I offer my sincere apologies for unintended shades of meaning. I only meant to say that you all have talents for persuasion. You speak well, as ambassadors must. But you can also describe what you believe should happen, and afterward others believe it as well. This is a powerful talent. I do encourage you to cultivate it, however much it may remind you of dangerously fickle people and abuses of authority."

Nadia turned away and muttered the word *politicians* again.

Gabe felt a sinking feeling as though someone had cranked up the gravity. Whatever the extra entanglement had accomplished, it had not increased Nadia's diplomatic skills. Pretty much the opposite.

The Blue Envoy politely withdrew, trailing a stream of apologies behind it. Then Speaker Tlatoani called out from across the chamber.

"Little mouths," she said. "Ambassadors."

"Great Speaker," Kaen answered with only slight impatience. "What have you decided?"

"Our faces have grown wide for you," the Speaker said.

"Translation help?" Gabe whispered.

"She's proud of us," Kaen whispered back.

Tlatoani went on. "If hidden Outlast considered it urgent to prevent your actions, then these actions must have merit. You should pursue them further. And the fleet cannot protect you, or protect ourselves by detaining you. Here this is understood. We the captains understand it. So the Terran ambassadors should both leave us, one for home and the other to meet with Machinae—if such a meeting can ever be possible."

Gabe drew himself up, and he spoke with formality—but he tried not to sound *too* formal, like a fraud, or an impostor, or his dad making fun of something with exaggerated pseudo-ceremony. *I'm not pretending to be an ambassador*, he reminded himself. *I am an ambassador. And their faces have grown wide for us.*

"You *did* protect us here," he said. "Thank you for that, and for your hospitality. I will always speak well of the Kaen."

"Thanks to you for the gift of ice and sanctuary," said the Great Speaker. "This system was ours before we were

Kaen, but now, as Kaen, it is not ours, and its resources are not ours to take. We survive by your guest gift, and we will speak well of you."

"What have the captains decided to do with the Outlast prisoner?" Kaen asked.

Qonne answered. "That thing will travel in a stasis cell with hatchling Kollontai. Two escorts will accompany it. One comes from my ship—a soldier and diplomat."

You're sending someone else to talk to the Machinae, Gabe realized. *You don't trust Nadia. You won't trust a hatchling to speak for us. But you are letting her leave. And Nadia is muttering to herself and ignoring all of you, so I kinda understand your lack of confidence.*

"My ship sends the other guard," said Mumwat, his deep voice muffled inside the purple bubble.

I hope they fix his suit soon, Gabe thought. *I need my envoy back.*

18

The three ambassadors left the House of Painted Books and returned to their small, temporary quarters in the academy.

Dr. Dromidan flew by to say something in Nadia's ear.

"I will," Nadia answered. "I promise. Even though I can't *actually* promise that. *Barnacle* might bounce off the lanes again, skip over several more decades, and arrive in some future galaxy empty of everyone but Outlast. That could still happen, you know."

Gabe winced.

Dromidan punched Nadia in the ear.

"Ow," she said. "Never mind. I didn't mean to say any of that aloud. I only meant to say yes, I'll be well. I promise. Nothing bad will happen."

The doctor whacked her ear again and then flew off.

The three ambassadors settled in to wait.

Barnacle still needed to feed—to refuel—with the cluster of Khelone ships who traveled in the fleet. And Gabe needed his envoy before Kaen could take him back down to Earth, as she had promised to do. So they waited. All three felt drained, exhausted, and unwilling to debate anything important. Gabe found a deck of cards in his emergency backpack and suggested a game instead.

"Interesting idea," Nadia said. "You do remember that I can't see any of the cards, right? The envoys rewired my head, but my eyes and my brain still aren't speaking to each other."

"Haven't forgotten," Gabe said while sorting cards. "But we could play Psychic. I'm ditching the face cards. Dealer draws one from the rest. The other two players have to guess which card."

Kaen watched him pick through the deck. "What do the black and red symbols mean?"

"Hearts, diamonds, clubs, and spades," Gabe said. "The four suits."

"Love, wealth, weapons, and work?" Kaen tried to clarify.

"Sort of," Gabe said. "Suits are important for other games, but not this one. Just guess a number between two and ten."

"Four," said Kaen.

"Not yet!" Gabe protested. "Wait until after I see the card. You're not trying to predict the future. You're trying to guess what number I'm looking at, *while* I'm looking at it."

Nadia made a thoughtful noise. "You're testing my extra, expanded entanglements. Think I might be a mind reader now?"

"Maybe," Gabe said. He shuffled the numbered cards. It felt satisfying between his fingertips. "They used all of us as points on a map when they remapped your brain, so maybe we're still linked. And if you can hear me thinking, then I'd really like to know about it, so I can think very carefully in your company."

Nadia laughed at him. And with him. Both at once. "Well, I can't hear your thoughts at the moment. Or anyone else's. Mine included. Everything's fuzzy. My brain feels like it's wading through waist-deep water in a thick fog. I can't focus on anything." Frustration threw off sparks underneath her voice. "This was supposed to expand my mind, and my sense of language. Not shut it down."

"Focus on this," Gabe suggested. "Just this. What card am I holding?"

"A seven," Nadia guessed.

"That's right!" Gabe said.

"No, it isn't," said Kaen. "That's a three. Unless the written numbers aren't translating properly. But I think they are. There's three of those small shovel symbols in the middle of the card."

Gabe winced.

Nadia's face and voice became coldly serious. "Ambassador Fuentes, are you cheating in my favor to boost my morale?"

"Maybe," he admitted. Back home he always played card games with Frankie, and sometimes Frankie needed to win. Gabe was used to cheating on a friend's behalf.

"Stop it," Nadia insisted. "Play the game. Pick another card."

They played the game, first tense and cautious with each other, and then finally relaxed and laughing. Every right answer *felt* like magic, even if it was really just random luck. And it did seem to be random luck. All three of them guessed the correct number *sometimes*— but usually not.

"I don't seem to be psychic," Nadia said, self-mocking and clearly disappointed underneath. "I don't feel like I have extra-special powers of Machinae speech, either."

Purple Envoy scootched through the doorway.

"Be patient," it said with the deep and grumbly voice that it always used with Nadia. "Your brain is still trying to understand its new shape. But it does seem to be working, I'm deeply relieved to say. I'm also relieved to report that Captain Mumwat is suited and mobile again. He was pleasant company, but I didn't otherwise enjoy my time serving as a fishbowl. The nutrient fluid had an unfortunate taste."

Gabe jumped up, thrilled to see his envoy. Then he sat down again, because it used that other voice. It spoke as *Nadia's* envoy, her friend and mentor, and not his own. He gathered up the cards and put them away.

Purple Envoy cleared its throat. "The Khelone ship has docked. They are waiting for you, Nadia. Time to say good-byes again."

"Feels like we just did," Nadia said. She poked the Envoy's sock-puppet face with one finger.

"It does," the Envoy agreed, "though it was forty years ago for me."

"Sorry about that," Nadia said. "I'll try not to lose any more decades this time. And I'm glad you gave my job to Fuentes. You picked a good one."

Gabe's morale improved instantly.

"I always do," the Envoy said. "Safe travels, Nadia."

"No such thing," she said. "Remember?"

"Instead there's trust," Gabe added.

"Very true," said the Envoy. "I'm glad you both listened."

Nadia Antonovna Kollontai held out one hand to her colleagues. Gabe took it. So did Kaen. This led to an awkward jumble of fifteen fingers.

"It was an honor to serve with you both," Nadia said before she let go.

The ambassadors traveled through Night by train car and corridor. Gabe walked with his jump bag on his back, his great-grandfather's cane sword in his hand, and the Envoy oozing at his feet. He looked around and tried to etch every visual detail into his memory; Night and Day above each other with the sun burning between them, Kaen of every species in the streets outside, and the honor guards who lined the corridors between the train stations and the docking bays. Many of the guards were human, but not all. Those with hands carried bright shields and shock spears. Hypnotic colors decorated each shield. Gabe found them distracting. That was probably the point. *Look at my shield!* he thought. *Don't notice the spear, not until after I zap you with it.*

Nadia left them to board the Khelone ship that waited for her. She had already said her good-byes, and offered no more of them.

I hope this works, Gabe thought as he watched her go. *You left our world and lost it to try this. I hope you don't lose any more decades when you try again. And if you can read my mind, then I hope you hear this now. Good luck.*

If she heard him, she did not react.

Gabe followed Kaen to her own shuttlecraft.

The phosphorescent wall lanterns of the welcoming airlock grew bright as they entered. This time the room did not stand empty. Two more soldiers, both bandaged, stepped forward to greet them—the same two who had fought the Outlast during Nadia's entanglement. The man had a bandaged throat, and said nothing. The woman spoke.

"Gabriel Sandro Fuentes, ambassador of our shared planet of origin, go in peace. More peace than you found here. Speak well of us wherever you go, but tell no one where we are, or where we are going."

Gabe tried to sound official. "Be welcome in this system, and go in peace when you leave for other suns." That sounded silly in his own ears rather than grandly important, but neither one of the adults laughed at him. Instead they stood at either side of the airlock, guarding one last passage through *Calendar*.

Kaen opened a storage locker in the wall. "Your old suit is here," she said. "But you're welcome to trade it for one of ours. Ours are less . . . bulky."

Gabe gladly traded the orange cosmonaut suit for

Kaen craftsmanship. Once suited up and helmeted, Kaen and Gabe climbed down into the shuttlecraft. The Envoy followed. It used its puppetlike mouth to catch each ladder rung as it went down.

"I'm surprised the captains aren't sending any soldiers along with us," Gabe said once the airlock closed behind them.

"Quiet that thought!" Kaen said quickly. "Don't speak it aloud, or it might still happen. We don't need anyone looming over us and having loud opinions. This craft is protection enough."

They settled into the back of the shuttle. Kaen steered the ship with gestures and with buttons on her bracelet. Gabe felt heavier as they launched, and then all sense of weight left him. He watched the projected images of fleet ships as they flew. He watched the flying saucer of the *Calendar* disappear behind them as they left the ice cave and Ceres behind.

"So where are we going, exactly?" Kaen asked as she set a course inward, toward the sun. "I'll take you down to the surface of the old homeworld, as promised. But planets are large. I assume you want me to bring you somewhere specific."

"I do," Gabe said. "Two places, if you're willing to take on the extra travel. We need to land in the place where

I'm from, but where I've never actually been, and pick up one more passenger."

"Who?" Kaen asked.

"My dad," Gabe told her.

He tried to explain his family's complicated circumstances, but the words *father* and *citizenship* both translated strangely. Families had very different shapes aboard *Calendar*. Kaen's uncles—her mother's brothers, specifically—were closer kin than her father. She usually lived at her uncle's farm in Day whenever she left the pyramid in Night. And while the fleet did have formal rules for individuals traveling between the ships, or for inviting new ships and civilizations to travel with them, such rules and guidelines sounded far more flexible than U.S. immigration law.

"I don't understand," said Kaen. "I hear your words, and I know what the words themselves mean, but I *still* don't understand. Migration is a fundamental right. Life moves. It travels from world to world, either in fleets of ships or as bacteria inside comets. *You* seem to know that already. You offered us sanctuary. You know what hospitality means between nomads. But your world doesn't."

"It's your world too," Gabe insisted.

"No," said Kaen. "I don't think it is." She tapped her

bracelet. A projection of the Earth enlarged to take up most of the shuttle. "Show me where we're going."

Gabe watched the world turn under him. Night covered the Americas. He pointed to a large and sprawling glow of city lights in southwestern Mexico. "Here."

Kaen seemed surprised. "Our ancestors left from that same part of the world."

"I know," Gabe said. "I kinda figured that out already."

They passed quickly through the solar system, over the Earth, and into thickening layers of atmosphere above the Pacific Ocean. Then Kaen steered them eastward, over the water, over the beaches and mountains of Central America, until the shuttle finally hovered above the bright lights of Guadalajara.

"Is this it?" Kaen asked. "Is this the City in the Valley of Stones?"

The projection covered the shuttlecraft floor. Kaen and Gabe loomed above Guadalajara like kaiju.

"I think so," Gabe said.

"It's almost as large as *Calendar*," said Kaen. "How will we find your uncle here?"

"Father," Gabe corrected. "He'll be at my grandparents' house. I have the address. He made sure all our jump bags included a full list of family contact info." He dug out the address book and paged through the entries. "Okay, here. The Fuentes family home. I don't know where this is, exactly. I wish I could google the address first to find out exactly where it is, but my phone isn't fancy enough."

Kaen tapped her bracelet. The projection shifted to include street names. Gabe even saw a little Google logo glowing in the corner.

"Your shuttle can read our Internet?" he asked, extremely surprised.

"Of course," she said. "It's just a trick of translation. And we are very good at translation." She glanced at his address book, and pushed more buttons. One house glowed.

"That's it?" Gabe asked.

"That's it," she answered. "But I don't see a workable landing site anywhere near. We'll have to leave the craft in the western hills, here, and then use a local vehicle to get closer."

"Okay," said Gabe. "We should be able to catch a bus. And a stealthy landing would probably be best."

"So we shouldn't expect a formal and ceremonial welcome for this world's absent ambassador?" Kaen asked.

"No," Gabe admitted. "The world didn't notice when I left it."

"Good," said Kaen. "Then we won't have to deal with the extra attention. I really don't mind spending time away from the captains." She gestured slowly and steered them into the surrounding mountains. "The world is turning back around to face sunlight now. Almost morning. Strange to see night and day switch places with each other."

One stolen and sinuous mining craft followed the ambassadors.

It had burrowed deep into ice and up through the surface of Ceres to leave undetected. Now it sped down gravity's slope toward the sun and the third planet.

The craft carried a single passenger, a single Outlast. He had sabotaged the artificial sun and remained far from the fight, still hidden, still waiting.

Now he studied the stars until he knew their relative positions, knew where this system turned inside a small spur of a spiral arm.

He knew where he was.

In that same moment every Outlast warship also knew.

19

Nadia Antonovna Kollontai climbed aboard the waiting Khelone ship. If an honor guard stood watch to either side, she did not notice them. *Barnacle's* airlock squeezed itself shut behind her.

The inside walls were smooth and curved, like the interior of a seashell. A Khelone ship was a living thing. The very first forms of life swam through space without stars or planets, when space itself was still warm and the stars had yet to pull themselves together. Then space gradually cooled, the stars grew bright and hot, and most life learned how to cluster there. But some adapted to the cold and never bothered to settle down in solar systems. Some living things remained nomadic, swimming through space, becoming their own ships. The Khelone, both the ships and their pilots, descended directly from those first forms of life that refused to hold still.

Nadia took in a breath that smelled leathery and familiar. She reached out and touched the smooth walls of the passageway, remembering what they looked like: opalescent, with light pulsing through them in rhythms more complex than breath or heartbeat. She remembered, but she couldn't see it happen.

"Hi, *Barnacle*," she said.

The wall grew briefly warm under her hand.

"I'm going to go looking for Rem," she said. "Help me find him. Warm means closer, and cold means farther away. Warm also means yes. Good plan?"

She felt another flash of warmth.

"Here we go."

Nadia climbed through the spiraling shape of the shell and into the central chamber. She recognized it by the way sound bounced away from the smooth dome overhead. She could also hear Rem tap against the floor with his toes and fingers, communicating with the ship. The tapping stopped.

"Welcome back aboard," said Rem.

He still sounded like Yuri Gagarin. He would have looked like Yuri Gagarin if Nadia could still make visual sense of his translated appearance. But he did not sound welcoming.

Nadia guessed why. "They brought the Outlast prisoner aboard, didn't they?"

"Yes," Rem told her. "One of those creepy, aloof, geno-cidal, territory-gobbling things is here. Along with two guards. The aquatic one is good company, and *Barnacle* might even agree to flood a single cabin so she can swim around without that big, galumphing suit of hers, but the beaked one struts, preens, and glares. I do not like having them aboard. *Barnacle* and I never agreed to take on more passengers. We certainly never agreed to transport *an Outlast.* Do you know how many Khelone clusters the Outlast have killed? You don't. You can't. Because no one does. We've lost count. And we've had to change all of our old migration patterns to avoid Outlast territory—our *ancient* migration patterns. Gone now. All of the trail markings gone. We used to drop bread crumbs, little food packets to mark our routes. They'd stay fresh, pre-served in the vacuum. Each ship would put special care into crafting bread crumbs. We'd code the flavors with information—velocity, intentions, destinations, maps, all sorts of important data. It's a gift, the most important gift. A bread crumb is hospitality and hello to whoever passes that way next, which might happen soon after-ward or a thousand generations later. If you explore new territory, somewhere the Khelone have never been before, then you leave the first set of crumbs behind. If you find an old one and eat it, then you always respond by leaving another in its place. That kept the routes steady and consistent. That maintained our long history. But then the Outlast figured out how to use the crumbs to track us down, or else leave deadly traps along our routes. They're killing us, and they're killing the oldest known historical records. We've stopped making new crumbs. The few I've found lately are coded with instructions for silence. *Whoever gets this, please savor it and do not drop another.*" Rem paused for breath. "And now we have an Outlast on board. This makes me so very unhappy."

"I'm sorry," Nadia said, and she was. "But it might help us get into the lanes, which might help us talk to Machinae, which might shut down the spreading Outlast completely."

"That's three *mights* I've counted," said Rem. "This represents significant levels of uncertainty. Plus I hear they've rearranged your brain shape. Sounds drastic. I'm relieved that you can still walk and talk."

"Likewise," Nadia said, her voice dry. "So far it's just given me a foggy headache."

"You inspire great confidence," said Rem.

"You don't need confidence," Nadia told him. "You are the greatest pilot in the galaxy. Confidence is for the self-deluded, or for those who avoid dangers and refuse risks. You're better than that. No other pilot whispered of in legend or coded into millennia-old bread crumbs has ever accomplished what you're about to do."

Nadia had met daredevil pilots before. She had met cosmonauts and the adolescent test pilots who wanted to become cosmonauts. She had met Yuri Gagarin and Valentina Tereshkova. Every single one of them loved flattery.

You're a politician, the Kaen envoy had said, and the word still stung even if it wasn't supposed to. Nadia wanted to argue with that word, but she couldn't.

Rem gave a mocking and affectionate laugh, a Muscovite laugh. Her flattery was obvious. It still worked. "You're full of noxious waste byproducts, human."

"Thank you," Nadia said. "Are we ready to launch?"

"Born ready," he told her. Nadia heard his toes and fingers tap against the floor and wall.

Barnacle pushed away from *Calendar*, away from Ceres, away from the Kaen fleet. The ship began to spin. The domed ceiling became a curved, concave floor as the spinning *Barnacle* made her own centrifugal gravity.

Nadia had loved their first launch, when they left the Zvezda base. She had been able to see at the time. Drastic shifts of gravity were unsettling to experience blind. She whacked into Rem when she found the new floor, and both of them said untranslatable things. Then

Nadia found somewhere to sit on the curved shell and tried to stay away from the pilot's tapping toes.

"We're clear of the asteroid belt," he said. "Time to take shortcuts."

"Try not to lose another forty years," Nadia suggested.

He didn't answer, which meant he had no attention to spare. Nadia dropped the joke and insult from her own voice.

"Tell me what you see," she asked. "Tell me what *Barnacle* sees."

Right at that moment the ship would be sharing an outside view across the curved shell around them. Nadia missed that view.

"She sees the lanes," Rem whispered back. "She sees a web of darkly shimmering strands. And she can feel gravity leaking into our dimension from other, stranger places."

Nadia held her breath. She held on to the single, brightly burning hope that she allowed herself to have. *This might work. It might. I left the world and lost the world to try it, and this time it might work.*

Barnacle twisted, flew, and fell into the lanes.

Gravity inside *Barnacle* got very weird.

Then it settled.

Nadia and Rem lay sprawled in the domed central chamber.

"Did it work?" Nadia asked. "Where are we?"

"Somewhere else," said Rem. He sounded more concerned than triumphant. "Somewhere entirely else. The space outside is . . . different. Thicker. More *viscous* than we're used to. It isn't a void, it's a dark and soupy swirl. Weird. I was expecting a network of tunnels burrowing through space-time. This is more like an ocean." Fingers and toes tapped against shell. "*Barnacle* is trying to get her bearings, but she can't make much sense of her senses yet. She's trying to tell me—"

Rem stopped talking, suddenly, so that he could scream instead.

"What?" Nadia demanded. "What was that? What's wrong?"

"I don't know," Rem told her. His words tumbled out fast and uncertain of each other. "I don't know what that was. Something just moved outside. Something massive. Something that might swallow us whole and not notice. *Barnacle* would very much like to turn around and bolt, but she hasn't figured out how." His taps against the shell made a steady, frantic rhythm. "We're caught in tides and currents, but I'm not sure if this is the direction we want to go—or if *direction* even means anything here."

Nadia wanted to see. She desperately wanted to see, more than she had while walking through the streets of Night, more than she had in the House of Painted Books or the Hall of Murals, and almost as much as she had while confined in the darkness of a kitchen cupboard.

Calm down, she told herself. *You don't spend most of your time upset that you can't fly or breathe underwater. You also can't see. Doesn't mean you're broken. Everyone just works with what they've got.*

Barnacle shivered and shook. Then she held extremely still.

"Now we're stuck," Rem reported. "The viscous liquid stuff pulled back to make a bubble around us. Then it solidified. We're stuck at the edge of the bubble as though half-frozen in ice."

"What should we do?" Nadia asked. "The Outlast can travel through this dimension somehow, so there must be a way."

"We did bring one with us," Rem pointed out. "Maybe we should ask how they manage."

A voice echoed through the ship. Nadia felt it as much as she heard it.

GREETINGS.

"Rem, did you hear that?" Nadia whispered.

"Hear what?" he asked.

GREETINGS, the voice repeated.

"Greetings to you," Nadia answered. "This is Ambassador Emeritus Nadia Antonovna Kollontai of Terra. Whom do I address?"

GREETINGS, said the voice, as though Nadia hadn't spoken at all.

"I still don't hear anything except you," said Rem.

"Maybe because you haven't had your brain rearranged the way I have," Nadia said. "I can hear someone out there, but they don't seem to be able to hear me."

GREETINGS.

"Okay," Nadia said. "Time to suit up. I need to go outside."

"I'll go with you," said Rem. "I should investigate our stuckedness and try to get us unstuck. But be careful. We don't know what the rules are here."

"I'm an ambassador," Nadia pointed out. "I'm very good at figuring out rules of conduct."

"I don't mean polite rules of conduct," said Rem. "I mean rules of *physics*. The Outlast skip over hundreds of thousands of light-years for freebies by moving through this place. So anything could happen. We might disappear, or explode, or turn into an ever-expanding and sentient nebulae stuck in one endless moment of pain. You might age a few million human lifetimes in one moment. Your feet might get older while your head gets younger. Who knows?"

"Who knows," Nadia agreed. "Maybe we'll transform into dozens of butterflies and bunny rabbits. Sure. We don't know what will happen. That's always true. We never, ever know what's going to happen next. So let's go find out."

GREETINGS.

Nadia stepped cautiously across the inside surface of the bubble in a borrowed Kaen suit, one that had never belonged to Valentina Tereshkova.

Her molecules hadn't torn apart in an ever-expanding nebulae of endless pain, or turned into bunnies, or experienced any other sudden consequence of unfamiliar physics.

"Talk to me," she said to Rem. "Tell me what you see."

Please, please, please, let the translation matrix still work out here, she thought.

It did. Rem spoke, and she understood him. "The stuff we're walking on looks like dark stone, semitransparent. Veins of some shimmering stuff run through it. Pale light pulses through those veins."

Nadia continued to walk across the stone-like surface. She felt gravity, or something similar. She felt as though she should be able to just push off and float, but she couldn't. Instead she took small and careful hop-steps, just as she had in her very first moonwalk before learning how to run there. She remembered moving across a frozen pond as a very small child, holding hands with Aunt Martina on one side and Uncle Konstantine on the other. She remembered staring down through clear, dark, solid pond water in wintertime, wondering where all the fish had gone, imagining all of them frozen in midswim. She remembered seeing bubbles trapped in the ice, and how they looked like tiny stars. It gave a sense of vast depth to small, frozen ponds.

Rem made a low, slow noise.

"What is it?" Nadia asked.

"Something is pushing its way up through the ground," he told her. "It looks like . . . it looks like a suit, a bulbous stone suit. It's moving toward us now, roughly you-sized and you-shaped, but . . ."

"But?" Nadia pressed.

"But I think the inside of that stone-suit is much larger than it looks from here. The rough helmet seems like it isn't any bigger than yours, but I can see something moving inside it. Something . . . far away. Now it's moving closer. Much closer. Now it's pressing itself up against the inside of that crystal helmet and opening one eye. That eye is bigger than the helmet itself."

"Am I facing toward it?" Nadia asked.

"Yes," Rem told her.

Nadia raised one hand. "Greetings? Hello?"

She heard no answer. She wondered what surrounded them. Air? Vacuum? Some other sort of gas-like stuff? Whatever it was, it didn't seem to carry sound.

"It's coming closer," said Rem, clearly alarmed, clearly trying not to be. "The eye is staring at you without blinking. Now it stopped. Now it's leaning forward. You should seriously consider backing away."

Nadia didn't move. "I think I know what it's doing. This is how cosmonauts talk without radio. If you touch visors then sound moves directly from one suit into the other."

She felt a small thunk against her helmet visor. Then she felt a voice pass through all the small bones of her face.

GREETINGS.

She blinked, and then grinned, and almost gave a gleeful shout.

"Greetings," she said. "I am Nadia of Terra. Are you of the Machinae?"

The voice changed and expanded.

What are your origins?

By what expansionist imperative have you spread so far beyond your habitat of origin?

How did you come to be here?

Do you travel here by accident or by deliberate intention?

What are your deliberate intentions?

How well do you treat the machines that you make?

What wavelengths of light are you able to perceive?

Do you strive to increase the number of possible outcomes radiating outward from any given nexus point?

Do you strive to decrease the number of possible outcomes radiating outward from any given nexus point?

What stories do you tell?

What games do you play?

Are you intelligent?

Are you alive?

The sound and the sense it carried overwhelmed her. Nadia felt like she was drowning in that voice, like she couldn't breathe while surrounded by it. Separate threads of meaning pulled her consciousness in every direction at once, and then she lost consciousness entirely.

20

Gabe found pesos in his emergency backpack. He also found Canadian currency, stashed there just in case the family needed to move even farther north, and he found a small, sealed envelope marked DO NOT OPEN UNLESS SURROUNDED BY GHOST PIRATES. Dad liked ghost stories and obsessed over emergency plans. Gabe searched for more envelopes that might prove useful in the event of genocidal alien invasion, but he didn't find any.

He dug out his set of spare clothes and gave them to Kaen. They set aside space suits and clothing woven out of space-grown corn silk, and they pulled on grubby and uncomfortable jean shorts and T-shirts instead.

"Have you visited any actual planets before?" he asked Kaen with his back turned, only slightly nervous about changing clothes in her company.

"Yes," she said behind him.

"What was that like?" he asked.

"Strange," she said. "Too big and too small at the same time. I kept looking up and feeling alone without a twin city overhead. But we didn't stay long."

"Why not?"

"Outlast."

She didn't elaborate. She didn't need to.

Gabe tried not to remember the clenching pressure of pale Outlast tentacles. He decided to bring the cane sword with him. It didn't look so very fancy while sheathed—just a walking stick with a metal tip.

Gabe stuck the pesos and the address book in his pocket. "Do you have a translator portable enough to bring with us?" he asked.

"Yes," said Kaen, and tapped her bracelet.

"Good," said Gabe. "Wait. Hang on. Why didn't you use that when we first met at Zvezda? Why did you force us to rely on our own patched-together translator?"

"I did use it," Kaen admitted. "I set it to receive, and not to transmit. It only worked for me. I wanted to test the measure of your welcome."

"Ah," Gabe said. "Smart."

"I thought so too."

They studied street views and bus routes projected onto the floor until Gabe felt like he had a solid sense of where they were and where they were going. Then Kaen spent some time reassuring the shuttle that they would be fine, and that they didn't need a massive and mechanical jaguar prowling through the city streets along with them.

"I should go with you, at least," the Envoy said.

"You're heavy," Gabe said. "I'd rather not lug you around this time. And we'll be fine. We're home!"

"You are in an unfamiliar sort of home, Ambassador," the Envoy said. "Go carefully, and hurry back."

The companions hiked down from the hills and into the city below. The air burned hot and dry around them, the same temperature as a Minnesotan summer day but with far less moisture.

Kaen kept glancing up at the sky.

The bus system turned out to be complicated. Each bus ticket cost six pesos, and the tickets didn't transfer, so when they switched buses they had to buy new tickets.

Once in town they passed La Minerva, a big, public statue of the Mediterranean goddess of wisdom and warriors. She looked like a soldier of the Kaen with shield and shock spear. Then they passed the statue again when they got lost, switched buses, and doubled back.

The ambassadors watched the world outside the bus window.

Gabe glanced sideways at Kaen. *I wonder what she sees. I wonder how strange this is to her. Probably not very strange. She knows how to move through alien worlds and civilizations. But this is the alien place that we both came from. And it's a little bit strange to me.*

Crowds of people flowed on and off the bus like water unsure about which way was down. A sunburned tourist sat across the aisle. He wore a shirt with an old stone calendar drawn on the front. Kaen stared.

"Ese dibujo se parece a mi nave," she said softly. Gabe heard the words in Spanish. He heard his own thoughts in Spanish here. "It looks like my ship and all the maps we make—maps of the whole galaxy with a massive black hole in the center, in the heart of the sky. We map out ourselves in that picture, suns and lives and generations."

"The face in the center is supposed to be the sun," Gabe said. "Our sun. The one in this system."

"Suns do like to be the center of attention," said Kaen. "Why is it sticking out its tongue?"

"Because it demands the constant sacrifice of blood and human hearts," Gabe said, channeling his mother's knowledge of archaeology.

Kaen looked shocked and skeptical. "Are you joking? Did that translate properly? Is that the sort of thing you do here?"

"No," Gabe said quickly. "Not anymore. It was an ancient Aztec thing. They added the face and the tongue to older Mayan calendars. And I'm pretty sure your ancestors left this system long before the Aztecs came conquering. Spaniards came conquering after that."

"Which are *your* ancestors?" Kaen asked him. "Those who lived here before, or the conquerors?"

"Both," Gabe said, uncomfortable.

The bus passed the Minerva statue one more time.

Gabe finally stood at the gate of his grandparents' house.

He peered through it at the paved courtyard embraced by the white-painted sides of a single-story house. The roof had a deck. He couldn't see anyone up on the deck or inside the courtyard.

"Your kin live here?" Kaen asked.

"Yes," said Gabe. "I've seen pictures. Talked on the phone. But I've never been here before, and I've never met them in person. I guess I could have called first. We could have stopped at a pay phone on the way. But I'm not sure what I would have said. 'Buenas días, Abuela. I just flew in from the asteroid belt. ¿Está mi papá aquí?'"

"Eres un embajador," Kaen reminded him. "You're an ambassador. Figure out what to say."

"Right." Gabe opened the gate, crossed the courtyard, and knocked on the door of la casa de sus abuelos.

His grandmother answered the door. She looked older than she did in pictures. "¿Sí?"

Gabe swallowed uncertainties. "Buenos días, Abuela. ¿Está mi papá aquí?"

Her eyes narrowed. "Gabriel?"

Gabe's grandmother sat them down in the kitchen, surrounded by bright pastel colors. She gave them each a cold soda in a glass with ice and a lemon wedge. Kaen wrinkled her nose at her first taste of the bubbly drink. Then Abuela put together cactus salad and ceviche. Her movements through the kitchen reminded Gabe of his father, who was not here.

"He's gone," she said. "You missed him. He already left."

Gabe felt his small and secret hope extinguish. "Where did he go?"

"He went north," Abuela said. She turned away and cut vegetables with short, sharp chops of a very sharp knife. Her voice had a similar edge to it. "He hired a coyote and raced for the border."

"Translation help?" Kaen whispered.

Gabe couldn't answer at first. *We're too late. He's not here. He's already gone.*

Kaen asked again. Gabe answered on autopilot, without thinking. He still couldn't think in straight lines. "A coyote is a guide. A secret, smuggling sort of guide. The word also means a small, hunting mammal. And a trickster hero in old stories." Part of him recognized the fact that he was babbling. "But she doesn't mean either of those things. She means guide. Someone who helps you walk north through the desert."

Abuela continued to cut vegetables into smaller and smaller pieces.

"He was supposed to be here," Gabe said, his voice louder—probably louder than he meant it to be. "We were going to come up with a plan."

"Yes," Abuela said. "He did plan to settle in here for a long visit and try to sort out his geographical troubles through more proper channels. But then *you* disappeared. Days ago. And he couldn't stay, not with you missing. So he set out for the border and the desert walk. Meanwhile you hopped a plane and came here? How old are you, little man? Seventeen? You couldn't have called first?"

I'm eleven, he thought. *You're getting me mixed up with Lupe. Probably because we never came to visit. We couldn't come to visit. We wouldn't have been able to cross the border to get back home.*

"No," he said. "I couldn't have called. I just had to come find him."

Abuela shook her head. "Impulsive, dramatic idiots. Both of you, your father and yourself. Introduce me to your friend, and then call your father to explain this foolishness. He took a cell phone with him." She dug a piece of paper from her pocket and set it on the table.

Gabe wasn't sure how to introduce his friend, but Kaen spoke first.

"I'm Citlalli," she said. "Mucho gusto en conocerla. It's wonderful to meet you, and you have a beautiful home." She soon coaxed Abuela into a long conversation without giving away otherworldly secrets.

Gabe took his father's new cell number to the landline in the next room. He picked up the phone and dialed. It rang several times. Gabe hung up and tried again. It rang and rang without voice mail, without the chance to leave a message, without his father on the other side. Gabe hung up. Then he phoned Lupe.

"Abuela?" his sister asked, whispering and hopeful. "¿Hay algunas noticias?"

"Hey," Gabe said.

Silence.

"I'm at work," Lupe said. "I need you to understand that I'm at work right now, at the restaurant, in the middle of the lunchtime rush. This is why I'm not roasting your eardrums with the most intensely violent profanity you have ever heard or will ever, ever hear. Where are you? Never mind. I know where you are. You're south of the border, because you used Grandma's phone to call me. How did you get there? Spaceship?"

"Yeah," Gabe admitted.

"I'm going to stab that purple alien with my sword. You still have my sword, right?"

"Of course," said Gabe. "Got it right here. The Envoy isn't an alien, though. And stabbing it won't do very much."

"Then I'll settle for stabbing you. Where have you been? Never mind. I don't care. And I have to go. Just get home by whatever immediate means you can manage. The sooner you get here, the fewer times I'll have to stab you."

"I miss you, too," he said. "Is . . . is Dad there?"

"No," she said. "I know that he might be . . . *on his way* . . . but lots can happen between there and here."

Those words had their own gravity. Gabe tried to steer clear of them. "How are Mom and the twins?"

"They'll be fine once you get home. They won't be fine

until then. So get yourself home." Lupe paused. Gabe thought she had hung up, but she hadn't yet. "How's the planet?"

"Still here," he told her.

"Good," she said. "Try not to leave it again. Come home."

This time she did hang up.

Gabe listened to the dial tone as though it were something he could understand.

Lunch was magnificent. Gabe barely noticed the food itself, though he did notice that Kaen seemed impressed by it.

Abuela softened when she saw how much pain he was in. "How long will you stay with us?" she asked.

"I have to leave again today," Gabe told her. He expected her to argue with him, but she just shook her head and called him an impulsive and dramatic idiot several more times. *She thinks I'm much older than I actually am*, he thought. *That helps.*

"I've waited years upon years for a visit from my grandchildren," Abuela told him. She built up a cathedral of guilt, stone by stone. "And now you stop by for lunch. I suppose I'll have to take what I can get. Bring your siblings and stay for more than one meal next time."

"I'm sorry," Gabe told her. "I'm so sorry. But I really do have to go. I have to . . . I have to fix this."

Abuela uttered a long litany of complaints about stubborn sons and grandsons and their inability to ever hold still.

"Stay for siesta, at least," she insisted. "Everything shuts down anyway. Come with me now and meet your grandfather."

Abuelo sat on a white leather couch that wasn't really white anymore, watching television. He turned off the TV and took Gabe's hand with both of his own. His skin was spotted heavily, and he had an astonishing number of wrinkles when he smiled. He couldn't speak. Gabe wasn't sure how much Abuelo understood, or if he had the slightest notion who Gabe was. But his grandfather did seem happy to see him. And he held the cane for one long moment before he gave it back.

"Pick up the phone the instant you get home," Abuela insisted at the door. She pressed cash into Gabe's hand. "I would drive you back to the airport, but we haven't owned a car in years. My eyes are bad. Traffic lights all look the same to me now. But you found your way here, so find your way back. Hurry. I'm sure your mother's hair has gone entirely gray by now. Call me when you get home, and call the very instant you hear from your father."

"I will," Gabe promised.

Mom's parents live here too, he thought. *I've never met them either. And I'm not going to meet them now. But I'll come back. I'll come back.*

After several cheek kisses and several more stones stacked lovingly on Abuela's cathedral of guilt, Kaen and Gabe walked back to the closest bus stop and waited.

"Citlalli?" Gabe asked.

"That really is my name," Kaen said. "You're welcome to know it, but don't use it much. And never in the Embassy. Not while I speak for the Kaen."

They watched a bus approach from far down the street.

"I'm sorry that your uncle wasn't here," she said.

"Father," Gabe corrected. "And we're not done looking for him yet."

The Envoy and the shuttlecraft computer had learned how to talk to each other while they fretted and waited for the two ambassadors to return. Now the Envoy and shuttle worked together and tried to track his father down.

"Here's his cell number," Gabe said. "He'll have the phone with him. Can you use it to find him?"

"I'm sure we can," the Envoy said with solemn confidence—though it became less and less confident as the day wore on.

Gabe paced and waited. Kaen suggested an Embassy visit, but Gabe found himself utterly unable to slip into the trance, so he took up pacing again.

"I am now sure we can't," the Envoy confessed. "Either his phone is no longer working or it is somewhere remote and unable to exchange information with the network of satellites that cell phones use."

"Then we should fly over the desert and search for him," Gabe said.

Kaen made a skeptical noise.

"This is your fault," he told her, voice louder than he meant it to be. "I wanted to come find him right away. We would have found him right away if you'd just brought me here like I asked. Like we *agreed*. If the captains hadn't kept me detained, then we could have gotten here sooner."

Kaen gave him a long look. "It is a large desert. This is a small ship. And if what you've told me about the border is true, then armed and suspicious people patrol that area. I would rather not meet such people. It would probably lead to diplomatic complications."

Gabe hated how right she was. He went back to pacing.

"You should return home and wait for him, as your grandmother suggested," the Envoy said. "That would be the most prudent course of action."

Gabe couldn't even imagine doing that. "He's missing because I went missing. He's lost because of me." He shifted blame away from Kaen and back onto himself, where it belonged. "I have to do something about that."

Kaen said nothing.

The Envoy and the shuttle spoke softly to each other.

Projections of translated information filled the floor and walls. Gabe barely noticed. He paced back and forth inside a towering cathedral of guilt until the Envoy cautiously scootched up to him.

"We may have found something," it said. "Your father's name is Octavio Fuentes? Age thirty-six?"

"That's him!" Gabe said. "Where is he?"

The Envoy took in a long breath. "Detained in Arizona. We found mention of him in an arrest report."

21

Kaen landed the shuttle among the trees and scrubland of southwestern Arizona.

They hiked through the hills on foot, just as they had hiked down from other hills in another country, only that morning. The Envoy went with them this time. Spiked plants stuck to its purple skin.

The sun set. The sun-scorched ground continued to radiate heat. Stars came out, more stars than Gabe had ever seen from the Earth before—but far fewer stars than he had seen from the dark side of the moon.

"Not far now," the Envoy said. "Just over the crest of the next hill."

They climbed the hill and looked down at the detention center: a warehouse surrounded by razor wire, illuminated with huge flood lamps and patrolled at the gates by armed soldiers.

Gabe searched for a way in. He searched for a way out. He found neither.

"Can you present yourself as ambassador and demand his release?" Kaen asked. "Or at least *negotiate* for his release?"

"No," Gabe said. The word fell from his mouth like a dropped brick. "No one knows I'm the ambassador."

"Difficult to represent a world if that world doesn't know about it," Kaen observed.

"Very," Gabe said.

The Envoy spoke kindly and cautiously. "Now you've seen this place. Now you understand that we cannot help your father, not at this moment, not for the duration of his detainment here. We must leave, and fly farther north to rejoin the rest of your family. You must be patient, Gabe, and we must leave."

Gabe said nothing. He stared at the lights and the wires and the gates. Then he turned away.

Five armed and uniformed men stood behind him.

Gabe and Kaen tried to run in opposite directions. This didn't work out very well. One of the soldiers tackled Gabe. Another grabbed Kaen by the arm.

Her bracelet broke in his grip.

Two more soldiers held weapons ready, but the fifth

raised both hands in an *everybody please calm down* sort of gesture.

"Easy, kids," he said. "Easy, now. What are you doing up here?"

Kaen said something rapid and outraged. None of it made sense to the soldiers, or to Gabe.

Her translator broke, he realized. *Sweet mango chutney, we are so completely screwed.*

The soldiers spoke to each other as though neither Gabe nor Kaen were actually there.

"That wasn't Spanish. *Was* that Spanish?"

"What did they do, break out of the center?"

"Nah. I think they just picked a very bad place to hop the border. Bad for them. Easy for us."

The soldiers all shouldered their weapons. Then they used plastic zip lines to tie Gabe's and Kaen's wrists behind their backs.

"Come on, kids. At least we don't have to take you far."

They marched down the hill—all but the unnoticed Envoy, who peeked up cautiously from a hole in the desert sand.

The two ambassadors sat in the detention center intake office. It was an ugly room. Fluorescent lights flickered overhead. A bored and sleepy-looking guard with a clip-board sat in front of them.

"We don't have any more room," she grumbled. "We're way over capacity already. I turned away an entire busload of unaccompanied Guatemalan toddlers this morning. And now they bring in two strays picked up right outside the door? We should just toss you back."

Gabe felt a small, bright spark of hope.

The guard noticed. "So you understand English," she said. "But your friend doesn't." She took notes. "I'll need to know your names, where you were born, how you crossed the border, and how long you've been in the United States." She repeated the question in rote and monotone Spanish.

Gabe felt the spark fade.

"Name?" the guard asked again. "¿Nombre?"

I am Gabriel Sandro Fuentes, he thought. *I am the ambassa-dor of Terra and all Terran life. And I happen to be a U.S. citizen already, thank you very much. I've got a xeroxed copy of my birth certificate in my backpack. Which is back inside the shuttlecraft. But it doesn't matter anyway, because Kaen has no papers and I'm not leaving her here. So you don't get to know who I am.*

"Kid, just tell me your name."

Gabe mixed together his own name and Zorro's. "Gabriel de la Vega."

"And yours?" she asked Kaen. "Name? ¿Nombre?"

Kaen said nothing.

"Citlalli," Gabe offered. "Se llama Citlalli Pulido."

The guard noticed Kaen respond to the name that was actually her own. "Good enough." She stood up from behind the desk. "Follow me. We'll finish your intake procedure in the morning."

The detention center was really just a warehouse. Chain-link fences split the one big room into separate sections, which made it look massive and claustrophobic at the same time. The air was dry and cold. Sunlight never baked the ground in here.

Many hundreds of kids covered the entire floor, trying to sleep. Silvery mylar blankets covered the kids.

Everybody in here is young, Gabe thought. *Really young. So where's Dad?*

Kaen and Gabe each got a folded mylar blanket of their own. Then they got separated, Kaen to the girls' half of the center and Gabe to bunk with the boys. They had no chance to speak first, and they wouldn't have understood each other anyway.

The guard shut Gabe into a small square of fenced-in floor. Gabe stepped over and around the other boys to reach an open stretch to lie in. Then he tried to get comfortable, but that wasn't really possible.

The smaller lump of blanket to his left was sobbing and trying to hide it. Gabe made a low shushing noise, the same noise he always made to comfort his twin toddler siblings. The younger kid snuggled up closer. His sob-hitched breathing turned to snores.

"You're good with the little ones," whispered the kid to the right, his Spanish thick with an accent Gabe didn't recognize. "Excellent. I nominate you for babysitting duty tomorrow."

I'll still be here tomorrow, Gabe realized with slow certainty. *I'll still be stuck behind warehouse walls and razor wire in the morning.*

"Tomorrow," he said. "Sure. I'll watch him."

The other kid stuck out a hand. "Gustavo. Call me Gus."

Gabe took it. "Gabriel. Call me Gabe."

"Let me give you a quick rundown of the place," Gus whispered. "This *could* wait until morning, but I'll probably get transferred in the morning. We get moved around a lot." He propped himself up on one elbow. "Okay, the first thing to know is that permisos are a lie. A bad rumor. Practically everyone in here comes believing that the U.S. grants children a permanent pass if we ask for sanctuary. But they don't. They just toss you back—fast if you're from Mexico, and slower if you hiked here from farther south, but either way they'll throw you out again. And the guards get angry if you ask them about permisos, so don't ask. Especially not Huppenthal. He's the worst. Tall white guy. Look for the name tag. If it says 'Huppenthal,' do everything you can to avoid him. Don't even make eye contact."

"Got it," Gabe whispered. "Avoid Huppenthal."

"And take care of little Tavo there. Especially if I get transferred tomorrow. Find somebody to take over watching him before you get yourself processed and transferred. He's tough. Made the crossing all by himself. They picked him up in Texas by the side of the road. But he's also three, and he has trouble sleeping. Usually. Nice to hear him snoring now."

"I'll watch him," Gabe promised. "His name's Tavo?"

"Octavio," Gus told him. "Little Octavio Fuentes."

It took all of Gabe's diplomatic skill to smile and nod rather than scream at the distant ceiling.

Octavio Fuentes. Three years old. That's thirty-six months, *not thirty-six* years. *Translation glitch. I came looking for Dad and found a toddler. Which means that Dad might still be free, still crossing over the coyote trails. That's the good news. But the bad news is that I'm a tremendous idiot. We're stuck. Kaen is going to hate me. I've created a serious intergalactic incident by getting another ambassador arrested.*

Gus rolled over and away. "Buenas noches, Gabe. Bienvenido a los Estados Unidos."

"Buenas noches," Gabe mumbled. "Welcome to the U.S.A."

He closed his eyes, slipped into a trance, and traveled.

"Be welcome, Ambassador."

"Greetings, Protocol. Is Kaen here?"

"Ambassador Kaen is currently entangled, and she is expecting you. Please proceed."

"Thank you, Protocol."

Gabe walked through the wide expanse of the Chancery, surrounded by the games and negotiations of his fellow ambassadors rather than fences and walls, armed guards and razor wire. He felt like he could breathe again. Then he wondered what he could possibly say to Kaen. Breathing became much more difficult.

One of the clouds shifted to make an arrow. It pointed *up*.

Gabe looked up. Flying ambassadors circled and soared above him. Most of them had wings. Gabe didn't.

"Okay, then," he said. "So now I need to learn how to fly. Does anyone else down here know how to fly?"

Many of his colleagues did, but their help was not helpful.

"It's not so much about wanting the sky as it is forgetting about the ground."

"Picture the way matter bends space, and change how

you see that shape. Just fall whichever direction you want to go."

"You want to fly? Why would anyone want to fly? The hidden and burrowing games are much better than all of that ball throwing and cloud hopping. Don't fly. Learn how to dig."

"Just think happy thoughts."

Gabe listened to several offerings of contradictory advice. Then he stood on tiptoes, clenched his hands, and focused hard on the clouds above. Nothing and more nothing happened.

"Learning how to breathe underwater was so much easier," he said to himself. "I already knew how to swim. I just needed to convince my lungs that they were far away and safe from drowning. But I can't fly, and my whole body knows it. I've got to convince every single part of me that I can."

"That sounds exhausting," Sapi said from somewhere above him. She dropped down lightly to the grass. "Stop arguing with all of your various bits. This is a dream, remember? You're dreaming an entangled dream. Haven't you ever dreamed about flying?"

"Hi, Sapi," Gabe said. "No, I haven't. Or maybe I have. I don't know. I never remembered my dreams before coming here."

"You poor, sad thing," Sapi said. "Well, come on. Kaen is waiting for us. The thing about a flying dream is that there aren't really any mechanics involved. No flapping limbs, no imaginary wings. Just movement and intention."

"That's what I've been trying to do!" Gabe protested. "But *intention* isn't producing much *movement*."

Sapi pressed all of her fingertips together. "Calm down, close your eyes, and hold both hands up in the air."

He did. "Now what?"

"Now shut up and be patient. I'll need to take a running start."

Gabe waited. He kept his eyes closed. Then Sapi grabbed both hands and pulled him into the sky.

Kaen sat waiting on the topmost cloud.

Sapi dropped Gabe beside her. He expected to sink through the mist and plummet back down to the Chancery floor. He tried very hard to expect the opposite, just in case his own expectations would determine what happened next.

He sank partway into the cloud before it felt solid enough to sit on. Mist swirled around him like slow fog creeping across graveyards in very old horror movies.

Star clusters filled half of their view above.

Absolutely nothing filled the other half.

"What is that?" he whispered.

"The heart of the sky," Kaen told him.

"The center of the galaxy," Sapi clarified. "This is the view from the Embassy, perched on the edge of the great, big, supermassive, Sagittarian black hole—the violent swirl of nothingness that we all spin around. And these stars are the oldest stars, all dead and dying. The first galactic civilizations started here. They ended here. They're all gone now, everything but the Embassy."

Gabe watched the riotous and overwhelming view. Long streams of fire erupted from suns while they consumed each other.

He glanced sideways at his friend.

"Hi, Kaen," he said.

"Hi, Gabe," she said.

"Are you okay?"

"I am deeply unimpressed with Terran hospitality," she said. "And those silvery blankets are useless. But yes, I'm fine otherwise."

"Good," Gabe said. "And I'm sorry. I'm such an idiot. You're used to traveling between suns, and I got you stuck in the middle of a petty border dispute in the desert."

"We'll find a way out again," Kaen said. "And if we don't, then Speaker Tlatoani will send more ships to find me."

"I hope it doesn't come to that," Gabe said, "much as

I love the idea of space Mexicans swooping down on Arizona."

"Then let's find a way out."

"Okay. Try to avoid a guard named Huppenthal in the meantime."

"How will I know any of their names?"

"They're wearing small name tags," Gabe explained. "Which you can't read without translation. Okay, then. Look for name tags clipped to the front of their uniforms, here. Avoid anyone whose name starts with the letter *H*. That's two parallel lines with one perpendicular line between them. Like this."

He made an *H* with his hands. Kaen copied it with her own.

"Understood," she said.

They watched the heart of the sky.

Sapi amused herself by sinking down into the cloud and popping up again in random places. Then she moved slowly closer to Gabe and Kaen and tapped both of their shoulders, hard.

"We have alarming company," she said.

Gabe looked where she pointed.

Omegan hovered at the edge of the cloud. He waited there, unsure of his welcome.

Sapi looked ready to flee. Kaen looked ready to fight.

"Wait," Gabe said. "Please wait. Let's find out what he wants."

Sapi punched his arm. "Ambassador Gabe, I am always impressed by your infinite stupidity."

"Please," Gabe said again.

"No," said Kaen. "Whatever he knows, the rest of the Outlast will learn."

"That is no longer true," Omegan said. He hovered cautiously closer. "I come alone. I speak alone. No one else watches through me. I represent no one other than myself."

"How?" Kaen demanded. "All Outlast overlap with each other."

"And the worst punishment that we have is to be severed from all others," Omegan explained. He kept his voice soft and low, but Gabe heard pain behind it. "This was my punishment. I told you about the lanes and how we move through them. I tried to warn you before the attack aboard *Calendar*. So I have been severed. I no longer qualify as a sentient person. They meant to cut me off from the Embassy as well, but that part of the punishment did not succeed. Obviously. I am still here. I come to you alone, in absolute solitude."

Kaen crossed her arms and spoke with effort. "We have no way to know whether or not you're telling the truth."

"Then tell me *nothing*," Omegan pleaded. "Make sure that I learn nothing more about you, or your location, or your capabilities. Listen instead. Listen to me. And understand that *I already know*. Our warships travel through the lanes, all of them together, all bound for the Terran system. They are coming for you. They are hunting the three human ambassadors, the three who seek to shut the lanes against us. One of you moves through the lanes now. They will hunt her down. Two of you are still in the Terran system. They will hunt you down. One single Outlast is *already* hunting you down. His name is Psain. He sabotaged the sun inside *Calendar* while others attacked you there. He remained hidden in the aftermath, and he followed you down to the planet. He will find you. He tracks the energy signature of your entanglements. And he was very close behind you when I became severed and isolated. I cannot see him now. I don't know where he is, but I'm sure he is close. Keep moving. Keep running. Don't let him find you. Leave the whole system behind if you can, because every one of our warships will be there soon."

PART FIVE
AMBASSADORS

22

Nadia woke. Darkness and silence spread around her like a solid, immovable thing.

"Rem?" she asked. "Hello? Are you there?"

The floor felt more smooth and level beneath her suit-gloved hands. She climbed to her feet. Then she opened her eyes, just to see what would happen.

Pale lights floated and flickered all around her. Nadia didn't understand what they were or what they meant. She closed her eyes again.

"Ambassador Emeritus Nadia Antonovna Kollontai," said a very familiar voice. "Be welcome."

"Protocol? Hi. Greetings. I've missed you. Am I in the Embassy now? I must be, since you never leave. I was in the Machinae lanes just a moment ago."

"You are likely still in the Machinae lanes," Protocol told her. "Your entanglement signal is fluctuating strangely.

And you are not using any single sensory remote to receive that signal, as the current ambassadors do. You are using *all* of the remotes. How strange. You currently perceive the untranslated Chancery."

"I'm not currently perceiving very much about my surroundings," Nadia said. "But this was the plan. Sort of. Not the Embassy visit, but borrowing everyone's signal and using them all to map out new and exciting synaptic pathways in the speech centers of my brain. I need to talk to the Machinae."

"And have you succeeded?" Protocol asked.

"No," Nadia said. "I did make contact. I got some sense of sentences and shades of meaning shooting off in all directions . . . but it knocked me unconscious. Now I'm here."

"Perhaps I can assist you," Protocol suggested. "It is my purpose to facilitate communication. And it would be gratifying if the Machinae sent me ambassadors again. They have not done so for a very long time. You might ask them, if you succeed."

"I'll ask," Nadia promised.

"Then I will adjust the remotes and allow you to borrow their signal pathways more easily. Please be patient."

Nadia waited and considered the idea of an untranslated Embassy. *No playground. No fields and forests and water and swooping, soaring games in the clouds. Just a big, dark, empty space filled with little lights, each one a remote carrying entangled, imaginary dreams. That's all this is.*

She shook her head and stamped hard on that thought. *No. Not true. Translation is never just wishes and lies. We aren't all wandering around pretending to understand each other. We do understand each other.*

Ambassadors moved through the vast expanse of the Chancery. Maybe the place looked very different to every one of them, but they still met, and spoke, and played, and understood.

"Brace yourself, Ambassador Emeritus."

"Poyekhali," Nadia said.

She opened her eyes and watched the swirling motion of ambassadors, unable to properly recognize the sight. The remotes did not resemble anything else. Then, suddenly, they looked like stars. And then every single one of them went nova.

23

"Am I understood?" Omegan asked, his voice small. "Am I believed? You must run. You must wake up now and run. Psain will find you soon."

"We can't run," Gabe said, his voice small. "We're trapped where we are now. Both of us. And my people are trapped. We can't leave this planet, or this system. We don't know how."

Kaen held her own wrist where her bracelet used to be.

She can't contact the fleet from here either, Gabe thought. *She can't tell them to leave now, to start running. They'll be trapped inside Ceres when the Outlast arrive.* He felt a thousand guilt knives stab his stomach.

"Then I regret what you will soon suffer," Omegan told them. "I should leave you now. I should not remind you further of the suffering to come."

"Wait!" Kaen called out.

Omegan waited, uncertain.

Kaen waved him closer. "Ambassador, please join us."

Gabe, Sapi, and Omegan himself all stared at Kaen.

"I am no longer an ambassador," Omegan finally said. "I do not represent my people, or speak on behalf of my people."

"Ambassador Omegan," Kaen said again, her voice solid and insistent. "I invite you to join us."

Omegan came to sit beside them.

"This is aaaaaawkwaaaaard," Sapi sang under her breath.

"Shush," said Kaen. "Ambassador, tell us more about Psain. Tell us what he's likely to do when he finds us."

Gabe woke. He lifted his head to peer through the dim light and the chain-link fences. He saw a sea of mylar blankets and sleeping kids. He saw two border patrol guards near the wall.

He closed his eyes to see the Embassy and stars dying in the galactic center. The transition came easily this time. He still felt the blanket and the hard floor beneath him. He also felt cold wisps of cloud against his face.

"Nothing," he said. "Kaen?"

"Nothing here," she said, her eyes still closed.

"We prefer to attack in overwhelming numbers," Omegan explained, "but Psain is alone. He must hunt for you alone. He will be cautious, and try to move unseen and unnoticed. He will come very close to you before striking."

"Then he might not be able to reach us," Gabe suggested. "We're stuck behind walls and razor wire at the moment."

"No," Omegan said. "Nothing about your immobility will be helpful. He will find a way to reach you."

Gabe woke. He looked around. He peered up at the distant ceiling to see if a tentacled Outlast slithered there between the fluorescent lights. Then he blinked and returned to the Embassy.

I'm getting better at quick transitions, at least, he noticed. *Raw terror is motivating.*

"Can you defend yourselves?" Omegan asked. "Hiding will not protect you, not while he can track the energy of your entanglements."

"Not really," Gabe said. He missed his cane sword, but he'd left it in the shuttlecraft. The border patrol would have confiscated it anyway. "I could throw my blanket at him, or try to make a whip out of shoelaces."

"Does your species have any native protections?" Omegan asked. "Tooth and claw? Venom and shell? I hope that you do."

"We mostly survive by cleverness," Gabe admitted.

Sapi punched his arm several times. "Then be clever!"

Right, Gabe thought. *Sure. Okay. I'll be clever. I will*

outwit another alien assassin. I'll fight him off with blankets and shoelaces.

He looked around the detention center. One border guard patrolled the hallway between fenced-in kennels of kids. Nothing else moved. Gabe lowered his head before the guard noticed him.

"Nothing yet," he told his colleagues. "Kaen?"

"Nothing," she said, her eyes still closed. "I see one soldier. Only one. There used to be more, but I'm not sure where they've gone. The girl beside me is dreaming about a river and swimming across it. She talks in her sleep."

Something tickled the back of Gabe's brain.

"You understand her?" he asked. "Kaen, how can you understand her? Did you learn Spanish already?"

Kaen's eyes snapped open. "Translation. Someone nearby is using a translator."

Gabe woke.

The border guard was closer now. He wore a stolen Kaen bracelet, and he leaned very far forward as he moved.

Gabe squinted and saw tentacles.

"He's here," Gabe said in both places. "He's here, and he's coming for me first."

The translated guard unlatched the gate.

Gabe stood up.

Other kids stirred at his feet.

"¿Qué tienes?" Gus asked.

"Shush," Gabe told him. "Stay down. Tranquilo. We aren't the aliens here."

The guard opened the gate. Electricity crackled across the chain-link fence from his fingertips.

"Greetings, Psain of the Outlast," Gabe said.

Psain leaned far forward. "This noise is not speech. I will not recognize the noise as speaking. And no one will threaten our dominion of the lanes."

Lightning burned across his hands.

Gabe tossed his blanket over the reaching hands and shoved. He was pretty sure mylar wouldn't conduct electricity. It didn't. The Outlast tried to hold him, to shock and strangle him, but the grasping hands held only the blanket. Gabe slipped through the gate and ran.

He heard Psain behind him. The translated sound fluctuated between thumping boots and slithering tentacles.

He heard a loud, metallic thump high above him.

He heard no alarms or adult voices, and saw the bodies of soldiers slumped against the wall as he ran by.

A voice shouted from across the warehouse, but he couldn't understand what it said.

He closed his eyes and ran harder.

"Gabe, can you hear me?"

Kaen's voice. She sat beside him in the Embassy, in the center of everything. He tried to answer. He was out of breath from running.

"Find a wide-open space," she told him.

"Isn't one," he gasped. "Kids and blankets cover most of the floor."

"Then *make* a wide-open space," she insisted. "Run for the middle. Now. Right now."

He ran between fences. Some kids cheered him on, their voices sleepy. Others taunted him. "¡No se escapa para nada, tonto!"

He reached the center of the warehouse, the widest place between fences. Basic toys like Frisbees and Hula-Hoops lay scattered on the floor between blinking children, barely awake.

"Everybody move!" Gabe shouted. "¡Muévense todos! ¡Contra la valla!"

Everybody moved.

Gabe stood alone in the center, winded. He tried to catch up to his own breath.

Psain of the Outlast approached slowly over empty blankets and discarded toys.

Gabe looked for Kaen, but couldn't find her among all the watching faces.

He closed his eyes.

"You're not alone," Kaen said beside him. "*We're* not alone. Listen."

Gabe heard metal bend and tear above him. He opened his eyes.

The jaguar-shaped shuttlecraft ripped the ceiling aside. It lunged through the hole, landed in a crouch, and opened the jaws of its front hatch. It did not roar. It had no need to roar. Instead it crushed Psain of the Outlast in its jaws.

24

Nadia slowly crawled back up to consciousness.

She heard Rem's translated voice buzzing in her helmet radio.

He sounds upset, she thought. *I wonder what he's upset about.*

"Get up," Rem said, over and over again, insistent.

Nadia got up. He tried to pull on her arm. She pulled back.

"Is the stone suit still here?" she asked.

"Yes," Rem said. "Right behind you, watching us with that single, massive eye. But it knocked you flat when you tried to talk to it, so let's keep our distance, please. Come on. Back to the ship we go."

"No." She pulled harder. "I have to try again."

Rem said several untranslatable things. Nadia understood them anyway.

He let go of her arm.

Nadia turned around. "Where is it?" She wished she could use a clicking noise to echolocate, but the clicks would just bounce inside her helmet.

"Right in front of you," Rem told her.

She reached out one hand, found the Machinae, and leaned forward to touch helmet visors.

"Greetings."

Greetings.

The meaning of that single word expanded.

Greetings. We give curious welcome. We do not expect you to answer. We do expect you to answer. We are unsure what to expect.

Greetings. This has never happened before. Our histories have noted no single event like this one. We are threatened by this interaction. We are intrigued by this interaction.

Greetings. We recognize you as biological. We recognize you as something that recombines itself to resist entropy. We recognize you as alive. We have not observed or interacted with biological life for immense and unfolding tangles of our history, long before this moment. We are unsure what to make of this moment. We are curious about the possibilities emerging from this moment. Tell us what you make of this moment.

Nadia listened. She understood. She spoke and made herself understood.

"I am an ambassador."

More words and meanings branched out and away from that single sentence:

"I am a Great Speaker, an emissary, a messenger, a supplicant. I find ways to communicate with others who are alien to me, and alien to each other. I am part of a galactic conversation. Thank you for joining me in this conversation."

More meanings unfolded—much more than Nadia had meant to say at first.

"I've come a long way to speak with you. I've endured many dangers to speak with you. I have something to ask you. I have something very important that I need you to do."

Oops, she thought. *I didn't mean to say all of that right away. I meant to lead up to it with some proper small talk first.*

The Machinae answered.

Ambassador. We recognize you as such. You speak for others. Many voices contract and narrow into one single and limited voice. This is strange to us. We prefer to follow an utterance outward, into whole hosts of branching meanings.

We are delighted that communication is possible between us. We are also disappointed that you want to narrow the possible outcomes of our conversation to one. You can hear a multitude of voices, but you are still single-minded. You pursue a single goal, like a single-celled biological organism searching for food. You want to reduce what this moment might become. You want to make a single request of us rather than remaining curious and open to emergent, unforeseen possibilities and outwardly rippling outcomes. You come to us with demands. You want only one thing. Disappointing. Narrowing. Narrow.

"Wait," Nadia called out before the Machinae could pull away. More meanings branched and spiraled away from that word. "Please consider what I ask of you. Please hear what it is, at least. Don't you want to know? Aren't you curious to find out what brought me here? Doesn't it interest you to know why my request is so singularly important?"

No. And yes. We are still disappointed. You are still single-minded. You can speak in many simultaneous directions but you seek to travel only one of them. Tell us if you must. Tell us what single destination you have in mind. We will humor you to hear it.

Nadia closed her eyes. *Think. Stay calm and think. Don't use lots of words to focus in on the one thing that I*

want to say. Use few words and branch out from there. They
seem to like that better.

She opened her eyes. "Outlast," she said, and she
tried to put everything she knew about them into that
word. *Genocides. Fanatics. Conquerors. Invaders. Intruders.*
Murderers.

Outlast. We have met them. Many of their ships are
here now, moving quickly and with single purpose. The
Outlast are even more singular in their focus, more single-
minded, more narrow. The Outlast intend to be the only
form of life remaining in the universe, but the universe
is far more vast than their intentions, and they notice
very little of it. Theirs is a closed system, not subject to
change. The Outlast make no attempt to speak to us.

"Stop them," Nadia said. "That is my single request.
Close the lanes to them. Don't let them get where they're
going. Don't let them travel so far and so fast."

Narrow. Again you ask us to close pathways and contract the possible. We are more interested in opening
new and branching possibilities. You ask us to restrict
travel. We enjoy travels and migrations. Why should we
restrict it in others, whatever their actions? What outcomes of your request might interest us?

Nadia paid close attention to each expanding ripple
of meaning. *They aren't just dismissing my request. This is*

a genuine question. Why should they care? I need to tell them why they should care. I need to explain to an utterly alien consciousness why genocide is bad. Okay, then.

"Understood," she said. "I understand and agree that I came here single-minded. That's like asking a question when you think you already know the answer. I understand your disappointment. I'm sorry to have disappointed you."

Focus, she thought. *Get to the point. No, don't get to the point—expand outward from a single point. Tell them why this is important in all directions at once.*

She didn't know where to start.

Then she did know, and resisted that starting point.

"Cupboard," she finally said. "Heavy boots outside it. Melting, dirty snow left behind."

Her meaning expanded. She told them what it was like to live always unsettled and waiting to disappear. She told them what it was like to watch someone else's narrow vision of existence contract until it ceased to include you. She made them hear the sound of heavy boots. She shared all the grief that she had turned her back on and ignored: the disappearance of her aunt and uncle, the empty apartment in Moscow, and the decades of lost time between the world she left and the world as it was now. She shared the swirling, destructive absence that she always felt in the center of her chest, the black hole that wound up her own personal galaxy, the source of every single thing she did.

Nadia realized that this devastating nothingness included its own embassy. She still had one secret hope: *Communication is possible. Communication is always possible. Understand this. Understand me. Please understand what I'm trying to tell you.*

The Machinae listened.

Nadia finished saying what she had to say: "Outlast. They have a narrowing, contracting, single-minded, single-species vision of the universe, and if you do nothing, then you help them create it. If you leave the lanes open to the Outlast, then you shut down all other branching possibilities. But if you shut the lanes to them, then you help create a rich and infinite variety of possible futures."

The Machinae pulled away, breaking contact.

Nadia almost fell over. She stumbled and caught herself on the stone suit in front of her.

It leaned slowly forward until their helmets touched again.

Yes.

That single word expanded to include everything.

25

The Envoy scootched around Outlast remains to climb down from the shuttlecraft.

"Greetings, Ambassador," it said. "We came as quickly as we could, and tried to find a subtle and unobtrusive way to reach you both. We were ultimately unable to employ any such subtlety. Are you well?"

"Hi, Envoy," Gabe said, his voice still winded. "I'm okay. Thank you."

He took stock of their surroundings. Most of the other kids kept their distance from the large and deadly metal cat in the middle of the warehouse, but about a third of the crowd drew cautiously closer.

Gabe closed his eyes. "Kaen?"

"Here," she said. "I'm here. I'll find you. We're crawling through broken fences and opening each gate and small kennel."

Gabe sat on the warehouse floor. He hugged his knees.

Then he stood up, moved through the crowd, and tried to keep everyone calm.

Every few minutes Gabe closed his eyes to glimpse the Embassy.

Sapi punched him joyfully in the shoulder, several times.

Kaen looked distracted and distant. She paid more attention to the jailbreak in progress than her entangled self.

Omegan spoke up, his voice hesitant. "I am relieved that Psain is dead. But others will come. Ask the Kaen fleet for asylum and evacuate your world, as many as you can. Hurry. Our warships speed through the lanes."

"Untrue," said Nadia Antonovna Kollontai. She pulled up a wisp of cloud to sit beside them, and kept both of her eyes tightly shut. "Well, part of that was true. Outlast warships *do* speed through the lanes in huge and over-whelming numbers—but none of them will ever leave. We have revoked their visas and travel permits. Thanks to you all for letting me borrow snippets of your signal to braid together one of my own. Not that you noticed. And please spread the word. The Outlast will never come conquering again." She brushed cloud wisps from her knees and waved. "Bye for now."

* * * *

Nadia gathered herself to herself after enjoying that dramatic disappearance.

"Time to go," she said.

"Very much time to go," Rem agreed. Nadia heard his fingers and toes tap against *Barnacle's* interior walls, communicating. "The bubble around us dissolved, so we're free to go. But lots and lots of Outlast are hurtling through the soupy space outside. Their ships are better at moving through this dimension than we are. They've had much more practice. We should be leaving now."

"Not quite yet," Nadia said, unconcerned. "Let's go talk to the prisoner."

Rem didn't want to talk to the prisoner. Neither did Qomm or Watti, the warriors who stood constant watch outside his stasis cell. But Nadia insisted, and time was short.

"I will not hear you," the prisoner said, translated voice stubborn and absolute in its refusal.

"I will be heard," Nadia answered. "Listen. This is your only opportunity to listen. You will never leave the lanes. You—all of you—are about to become as alone as you've always imagined. Congratulations. I hope you find something interesting to do with yourselves from now on, until the universe collapses. You could try to conquer the Machinae. I don't recommend it, but I am amused by that idea. It would not go well for you. I suggest learning how to speak with them instead."

"There is no speech or understanding outside the Outlast," the prisoner insisted.

"Have fun talking to yourselves, then," Nadia said. "We'll be tossing your stasis cell through the airlock now. Your warships will come pick you up. Or else they won't. Either way, I have delivered my message."

Nadia turned away and left, one hand trailing along the smooth shell wall. She heard Rem catch up to her.

"Where to?" he asked.

"We'll need to bring Qomm and Watti home," Nadia said. "We should rendezvous with their fleet."

"That brings us back to your own home system." Rem sounded reluctant to point this out. Nadia felt tremendously relieved to hear that reluctance. "Will I be dropping you off too?"

"Not unless you insist on it." Nadia pressed her full palm against the shell. She felt warmth and welcome there. "It's not the same world as the one I left. I'd rather go looking for bread crumbs."

Kaen finally found the center of the warehouse through the maze of gates and fences.

She took the bracelet from Psain's arm. It was still intact—both the bracelet and the arm—though the rest of Psain was less intact. She raised her translated voice to address everyone.

"I am Ambassador Citlalli of the Kaen, and this ship is mine. I offer all of you asylum among the Kaen. If you have no people here, no one to look for you, no one to find, then come travel with me. If you wish to stay on this world, then take water with you and start walking. Look out for each other. If you would rather travel between worlds, among those who understand the rights of migration and nomadic hospitality, then wait in the hills outside. I have sent for transport. More ships will land here soon."

Mutters and whispers spread through the gathered crowd. Most sounded nervous, reluctant, and confused, but many others were hopeful, curious, and able to cope with their own astonishment.

Gus and Tavo came to stand beside Gabe. "How do we even get to the hills outside?" Gus asked.

"Just follow us," Gabe told him.

The shuttle moved across the floor. Chain-link fences broke like cobwebs. Its passage crumbled the outer wall and flattened the razor wire beyond it.

Gabe and Kaen walked out into the desert. He looked

up. He saw neighboring stars burn alone. He saw distant stars burn together across the horizontal sweep of the galaxy viewed sideways. He looked behind them to see kids leaving in clumps and clusters. Teenagers carried infants. Most of the kids scattered in every other direction, but some young nomads—Gus and Tavo among them—trailed behind the two ambassadors and followed where they led.

26

Gabe, Kaen, and the Envoy traveled north. The moon-lit landscape shifted from desert to farmland and forest beneath them.

"Almost home," the Envoy said.

"Almost home," Gabe agreed.

He had an idea, a secret hope, and it burned spark-bright inside him. He was afraid to say any part of it aloud, just in case his own voice would snuff it out. But he couldn't keep it to himself, either.

"Envoy?" he asked, finally. "You found an arrest record for little Tavo Fuentes, before."

"I'm so very sorry that he was the wrong Octavio," the Envoy said, mortified. "I should have scrutinized that information more closely. My negligence put you both in danger."

"I put us in danger," Gabe insisted. "It wasn't your fault,

not at all. And now little Tavo gets to travel with the Kaen. But can you dig deeper? Can you find networked information that isn't necessarily public, like Dad's original arrest and immigration records?"

"Certainly," the Envoy said. "Those who collect this information and restrict its use would call our access code breaking, and would be very upset by it. But this is simply translation. The Kaen are astonishingly good at translation." It pushed buttons on the wall and spoke to the ship. Glowing text scrolled through the air.

Gabe read his father's file. He double-checked the birth date and details of the arrest report. "That's him. Can we change any of this information from here?"

"Yes . . . ," the Envoy said, uncertain.

"Good," Gabe said. "Pull up Mom's record next, and Lupe's. Or make one for Lupe if it isn't there already. We need to add Frankie's house as the temporary home address for all of them."

"Are you sure?" the Envoy asked, a concerned shade of purple. "Is it wise to reveal this information? Your family is in hiding."

"I'm sure," Gabe said. "We won't need to hide after this."

"What are you trying to do?" Kaen asked.

Gabe stood tall and switched over to his formal, talking-to-Protocol voice.

"As the representative of this planet—all of it—I, Ambassador Gabriel Sandro Fuentes, invoke diplomatic immunity. I hereby grant citizenship within the United States of America to Lupe, Isabelle, and Octavio Fuentes. Please send them certificates immediately."

The shuttle soared low over south Minneapolis. It circled a public park, landed beside the baseball diamond, and crouched in the grass. Its mouth yawned open. Gabe came out yawning. He hadn't gotten very much sleep. Everything looked pale and gray in the early dawn light.

The Envoy crawled sleepily inside his backpack. Gabe hoisted it over one shoulder and took up the sword cane.

Kaen stood beside him. "Nice place."

"Thanks," he said. "Come visit sometime."

"I might. Our old migration cycle takes thousands of homeworld years to revisit the same sun . . . but the Outlast broke our old cycle. I don't know where we'll go now."

Gabe didn't know what to say, so he fell back on ordinary things that everyone says. "Safe travels."

"No such thing," Kaen reminded him. "There's only trust."

She pressed her forehead against his.

"I'll see you soon," Gabe promised. "See you in the Embassy."

"I will see you in the heart of the sky."

She went back inside. The shuttlecraft closed its jaws and launched.

Gabe set out through the park.

He passed the duck pond that Noemi kept trying to fling herself into. He passed the basketball court and small playground, all empty and silent in the early morning. The cane's metal tip made a clacking sound against the sidewalk.

Frankie's backyard was still a mess, the grass scorched from a failed model rocket launch and the blast of an orbital ice-mining drill.

The back door was open.

He smelled his father's cooking through the screen.

He heard his father singing at the stove.

"Todengeeeeeee dam magaaaaaaar tera saath na chhodengeeeeeeeeee."

Lupe and Mom sat close beside each other at the kitchen table. Garuda the iguana lounged across Lupe's shoulders. Zora the bird stood on top of Mom's head.

The twins sat on the floor and wrestled with Sir Toby the fox. Frankie sat there with him, playing with the twins, *helping* with the twins, even though Frankie was usually useless at this hour of the morning and *definitely* useless at watching the twins. His parents must have put him on a plane and sent him right back from California. To be helpful. And he was actually helping.

Dad served up something fried and spicy with a wooden spoon and saucepan.

The Envoy made a gurgling noise from inside the backpack.

"Shhhh," Gabe whispered. He remained just outside the kitchen door. "We're almost home."

Acknowledgments

Most of the following acknowledgments are also written into the back of *Ambassador*. This book shares the same debts.

Thanks to Guillermo Alexander, Kay Alexander, Bethany Aronoff, Kel Darling, Leonora Dodge, Sara Logan, Sasha Sakurets, Kathryn Sharpe, Joy Nelson, and Tim Hart for their knowledge of immigration law, social services, secret railroads, Russian translations, Mexico, Guadalajara, quantum physics, and cane swords.

Thanks to Melon Wedick, Jon Stockdale, Ivan Bialostosky, Nathan Clough, Haddayr Copley-Woods, Barth Anderson, David Schwartz, Stacy Thieszen, and Karen Meisner for their insights, critiques, and support. Thanks to the Blue Ox for the coffee. They make a mean cortado.

Thanks to everyone at McElderry Books and BG Literary, most especially Karen Wojtyla, Annie Nybo, Michael McCartney, Ksenia Winnicki, Joe Monti,

Tricia Ready, and Barry Goldblatt. My name is the one sprawled across the front cover, but publishing is a collaborative art.

Thanks to everyone at Simon & Schuster Audio for the audiobook production. I do love to read aloud.

Thanks to Carlos Fuentes, Sandra Cisneros, Gene Roddenberry, and Ursula K. Le Guin for their stories of the borderlands.

Thanks to Junot Díaz for saying this: "If you want to make a human being into a monster, deny them, at the cultural level, any reflection of themselves."

Thanks to Alice for uncountable things.